JAMES MACKEN

Wh

and optimism following several sudden and untimely young deaths within his circle of friends and family, including those of his fiancée and sister, James started writing short stories in an attempt to define and crystallise his feelings.

Readers, regardless of their religions or belief systems, found themselves exploring their own responses towards his stories in which tricky concepts - death, life, personal accountability, fulfilment of purpose - were fascinatingly intertwined. With encouragement, feedback and support from them, those stories led to **'Seven for a Secret'** - a timeless, magical adventure, provoking intriguing perspectives on why we are where we are in life.

During two decades as a teacher and performance coach, James has delivered hundreds of talks and workshops around the world, accumulating a hoard of insights into the challenges and choices associated with personal achievement and peak performance.

He is committed to the work of Amnesty International and speaks regularly in schools and colleges around the UK on their behalf.

James divides his writing time between the UK and South France.

"Who, reading this, has never been a child? Who here has never pondered over questions like 'How did I come to be?' or 'Why do people die?', 'Where do they go?', 'What is my purpose in life?', 'How do I know I'm on the right track?', 'How will I know when I've arrived?', 'What happens if I don't'. Matters of life and death can seem so confusing and contradictory. The good news is…after reading SEVEN FOR A SECRET, it doesn't have to be like that any more."

Dr. Michael Scott

Author of 'The Quest of Oswin Anfortas'

Seven for a Secret

By

James Mackenzie Wright

Seven For A Secret

Fisher King Publishing
The Studio, Arthington Lane,
Pool-in-Wharfedale,
LS21 1JZ.
England.

ISBN: 978-1-906377-00-7

Printed by Print Vision

Seven For A Secret

Contents

Acknowledgements

…for all inspirational souls

braving yet another

bash at life,

especially…

Rory, Daniel, Aron, Thomas,

Georgia, Isabella, Romain, Marwen,

Sadri, Adam, Clara, Shemsa,

Marie-Lou, Timothé, Sarah, Christopher,

Rosie, Billy, Poppy,

Holly, George, Jamie,

Olivia, Richard, Simon,

Josh, Ricky, Aaliyah,

Yazmin, Aurora, Oliver, Hermione,

Chloe, Tom, Alfie, Bea…

…and for those who'll choose their

next moments all in good time…

…George, Sophie,

Vinod, Hannah, Javier, Craig,

Roger, Rick, Phil, Andy,

Ruth, Jenny

and you, Helen

It's over 60 years since Saint-Exupery's Little Prince asked him to draw him a sheep. Of the many attempts he made, the one which pleased the Prince the most was the one where no sheep was visible, being as it was, inside a box. Some wise friends of mine, high in the mountains of France, reminded me that young people have the purest illustrations already present in their unclouded minds.

Far better not to impose the limits of choosing a single artist's images to accompany a story that expounds the concepts of limit*less* possibilities and *infinite* personal choice, they said, and I am persuaded that they are exactly right. I am really grateful to you, Nadia, Marc, Christophe, Elisabeth for that insight. What could be more personal for all of us young souls than capturing our own pictures and interpretations, illustrating what the book's philosophies, messages, and characters have conjured up for us?

Reading is freedom: freedom to bring our own insights of our own worlds to bear on the text of whatever book is currently in front of our eyes. Writing likewise - the fact that this story doesn't fit easily with mainstream western thinking is the whole point of writing it. We all find ourselves most naturally when left to discover our own paths.

SEVEN FOR A SECRET is a story. Perhaps a provocative one for some, given its themes and settings, but a story nonetheless, and like any story it is intended simply to be experienced and internalised. As you experience it we invite you to notice the thoughts appearing in your minds and to capture them in whatever form you choose. Send us your thoughts and pictures if you'd like - we reproduce a number of them on our website www.sevenforasecret.org.uk where we also log events and activities concerning the book's messages.

Despite the fact that writing can be a very solitary activity, it is far from the truth to say the same of producing a book. I'd like to thank many people for their support, encouragement, insights, wisdom and hard work in bringing this book alive. Particular thanks to Judy Cole for your inspirational courage, Chrissie Allan of Leeds Metropolitan University for your huge energies and unconditional support and Carol Wilson of Performance Coach Training Ltd for continuing to be the perfect coach. Rick Armstrong of Fisher King Publishing, you are a natural motivator and wise mentor - since the first meeting you have selflessly and tirelessly driven this project forward and I continue to be profoundly grateful for your guidance. Thanks also to

Rachell Weeks – Editor-US of Fisher King Publishing, Vivian and Ellie Wright and all my friends and family who have contributed kindly and sensitively in so many ways.

Lastly, it is you, the reader, to whom I reserve the final expression of gratitude, for having found this book and chosen to open it. I believe the portals of adventure swing open at precisely the same moment we find ourselves ready to explore behind them, so it is with great excitement and anticipation that I hand SEVEN FOR A SECRET...

...over to you.

JMW

Chapter 1

Helen's Anniversary

Mum had organised a party for Helen's anniversary and for her nearly-birthday too. She would have been twenty-one on Tuesday. That's why so many people were at the house today, although Holly didn't really want to stay around them because no one seemed to be having much fun. And everyone kept talking to her or asking her if she was all right, so she couldn't sneak upstairs to her bedroom to read her books as she would have preferred.

George, her little brother who was seven, was also bored. Two of his friends had been at the party till tea-time but their parents had picked them up over an hour ago so he had no-one his age to play with either. Dad always said that when you have two numbers in your age, that was when you really started being a grown up, so whenever anyone asked his age, George told everyone he was seven and nearly ten.

Most of the time Holly thought it was fun to have a little brother around. He could always make her laugh with his mad-cap stories which he could just invent on the spot. He had an amazing imagination and he was very generous, except when it came to sharing sweets with anyone. With anyone except Helen that is. Somehow she'd always managed to get him to share them, and she didn't even really like sweets that much, so she often gave them to Holly anyway when George wasn't looking.

When they both used to go to All Souls Junior School together, Holly used to keep a big-sisterly eye on George, but now she was at Lakeside Middle School she had made a lot of new friends and didn't see so much of him. Anyway, he was starting to find out how to be a real pain sometimes. He thought it was funny to do really gross things, like the time he left live worms in a margarine tub under her bed sheets, or put the class rabbit's droppings in her school pencil case.

Boys can be so disgusting, she thought, but she was always working out new ways to get revenge. Trouble was, the more ingenious her plans for revenge were, the more it seemed to feed his imagination, and he kept coming up with even worse pranks for the next time.

Holly watched him for a few moments. He was absorbed in a make-believe game with his favourite toys – some beautifully hand-painted tin tanks and soldiers that their Granddad had played with when he was a boy. He sat on the floor behind the dining room table. She had a sudden urge to join in, and take her mind off all the gloomy adults too. As she squatted down next to him she noticed that there were several tin soldiers wedged down to their waists in two slices of chocolate gateau. George was busy popping grapes over their heads, one by one.

"What are you doing, you little freakoid?!" she asked him, shaking her head in an 'I-always-knew-you-were-weird-but-now-you've-gone-completely-bonkers' sort of way.

George looked up, noticing her for the first time. "They're prisoners so you have to half bury them in mud and blindfold them so they can't see or run away," he told her matter-of-factly. "That's what they did in the old days."

"That's so gross," she said, thinking of all the bugs and insects that would bite the prisoners underground. George's prisoners looked weirdly, like aliens, with their skinny tin bodies and big bulbous grape heads. "Anyway," she stated authoritatively, "your prisoners would suffocate, so that would make you a murderer. A Cruel Freakoid Murderer!"

"Get lost, Teaspoon Head!" returned George, evenly, without looking up this time.

"Teaspoon Head??!" repeated Holly, grinning mischievously now. "You get lost, you... Cheese Grater Brain!"

"Corkscrew-Nosed Stinky Gloop!"

"Puff-Cheeked Bug-Eyed Larva Carcass!"

3

"Holly! George! Stop behaving like children and come and talk to our guests." Dad arrived just in time.

"But he is a child," piped up Holly, cheekily.

"Speak for yourself, Ugly Ancient Wart Witch."

"Baby Face Chimpo-Lips."

"Enough silly zonking, you two," said Dad trying to be strict but smiling all the same. "You can do something useful like help me serve some food in the other room."

Zonking had become almost a daily game and both Holly and George were expert at it. The only rules were no repetition and no hesitation. You had to think of new insults all the time, and you had to reply immediately – stopping to think or saying 'errr…' wasn't allowed.

If you did, the other person called you "Zonko" in the weirdest voice they could invent and you were the loser. Except that their games normally continued long after one of them had been zonko-ed, because neither of them would ever agree that they had hesitated, or used the same insult words twice. Helen used to make up rhymes and nicknames for most people she met, which was how she had invented zonking a couple of years ago. Back then she nearly always won, but now, after a lot of practice, (too much practice in Dad's opinion,) Holly and George were probably the best in their schools.

4

Behind Dad's back George was quietly mouthing "Bogey-faced Donkey-breath Slug Mucus" at Holly but Dad turned and saw him, and held up a warning finger. Holly saw her chance and mouthed "Zonko" at George for hesitating, and just got away with it before Dad turned back towards her too, with a poor attempt at a stern expression on his kindly face.

George stuck his tongue out at Holly and shrugged nonchalantly, turning his back on both of them. He resumed occupying himself with his grape-headed gateau-gunged prisoners of war.

Dad was hopeless at zonking…well the truth was that he never had a bad word to say about anyone, so to try and find instant insults as a game was beyond him. Helen used to tease him with some fabulous phrases, but she made sure she stayed *almost* out of his earshot so only Holly and George, (and occasionally Mum) could properly hear what she called him. Holly and George would be doubled up with laughter as she stage-whispered her best insults in his direction. Mum would try to pretend that she didn't find it funny but everyone knew why she kept excusing herself to go into the kitchen with the biggest smile creeping over her face.

Holly stood up and looked around the room again. Same old gloomy faces, same old subdued conversations. She picked up a cheese sandwich from the dining table and nibbled half-heartedly on it. Yesterday she had helped Mum to cook loads of food for the party, but today she wasn't really enjoying eating it. Everyone seems so *down*, she thought. Helen would have brightened things up if she could have been here. She'd be singing, doing silly dances and making faces – she loved showing off and making people laugh.

But that was the whole point.

Helen couldn't be here, and no matter how many times Holly had wished for her to come back, she had gone to …to… well, where did you go when you died? So that, as Mum had told her, was that. In fact the precise reason all these people *were* here was because Helen *wasn't.*

She hadn't even been ill or anything. A year ago she'd come back from the shops two days before her twentieth birthday and complained she felt dizzy. She'd lain on the cushions on the living room floor in front of the TV, and fallen unconscious. At the hospital, they couldn't make her breathe by herself again and she had just, well – died. Holly still couldn't really understand it. How scary that people could just die like that. Young people even. The doctors used some long words to explain what happened to her heart but as far as Holly was concerned, she had lost her big sister, life didn't make sense and it wasn't fair.

She was about to walk through into the kitchen, when all of a sudden, across the other side of the living-room, she saw a pretty young woman with a round, friendly face whom she hadn't noticed before.

In fact, amongst all the sad faces in the house, this woman seemed to be the only person smiling. A really happy, warm, smile and straight at Holly too. What is she smiling about, Holly wondered? Is she smiling at me? What's so funny? She looked around and behind her in case someone else was doing something for the woman to smile at, but no, everyone was talking in low voices and looking very serious.

Holly slowly walked around the back of the sofa, closer and closer to the woman, who never stopped smiling. As she drew nearer, she started feeling a bit nervous, but the woman's warm, kind eyes were still smiling at her and following her round the room. She couldn't take her eyes off the woman, even though she knew it was rude to stare, but deep down, Holly knew the woman didn't mind her curiosity.

Then she heard Mum calling her name and she looked round. Mum was beckoning her to come back to the table and was holding out her hands. Holly walked over and took Mum's hands but she wanted to turn away and go back towards the smiley woman. She turned her head to look…but the woman had disappeared. She was nowhere to be seen.

"You OK, Hols?" Mum was asking, and then some more questions after that, but Holly wasn't really listening because she was wondering how someone could just disappear like that.

"I'm fine, Mum," replied Holly politely, "um…is it OK if I go outside in the garden for a while?"

"Of course you can, sweetie, don't be too long," said Mum. "We are going to cut the big cake with candles on it soon. You can light them if you want."

Holly could see tears in Mum's eyes, and she knew her Mum could do with a really big hug. However, she was so curious to find out about where the woman had disappeared to that she just said "OK, Mum, see you later," and walked quickly away towards the chair in which the woman had been sitting.

On the seat of the armchair, where the woman had been just a few moments earlier, was a little pile of honeysuckle blossom. In front of the chair were several more petals, and Holly now noticed a thin trail of blossom on the floor that seemed to be leading out into the garden.

Funny, Holly thought. No-one else seemed to have

noticed the smiley woman, and even if they had, they seemed unaware that she had simply disappeared into thin air. Nor, she observed, had anyone noticed the honeysuckle blossom on the chair and on the floor. Holly made up her mind in a flash. She slowly sat on the edge of the chair for a couple of seconds, looked around nonchalantly before standing up again, scooping up a double handful of yellow petals and thrusting them into her jeans pocket. Then she walked straight through the French doors that led into the garden, trying her best not to attract anyone's attention.

CHAPTER 2

The Poppy Tree

A s soon as she was outside, she walked quickly to her favourite tree: the old horse chestnut near the back fence. Slipping a glance over her shoulder, she climbed into its lower branches and round to the other side of the trunk where no-one would be able to see her from the house. She pulled out a handful of honeysuckle blossom from her pocket and let it cascade through her fingers like wedding confetti. It settled on the thick gnarled branch by her feet.

Holly loved this old tree. She had nicknamed it her 'Poppy Tree' and the name had stuck. The whole family called it the Poppy Tree now. When people asked her what was special about it she told them it was her 'Place of Potential and Possibility,' or 'PoPPy' for short. It was the place where she liked to come when she needed inspiration about things. Everybody needs a 'Place of Potential and Possibility' she used to tell them, a place to sit and think, quietly, all by themselves where no-one comes to bother them, and this tree was her special, thinking place. She had sat and thought and planned things up here over the years since she had been tall enough to climb it unaided.

11

This evening she could only think about one person: Helen. Dad had found it really hard to accept that his daughter had died and hardly ever mentioned Helen's name around the house. Helen was born into his previous marriage that had only lasted four years. His first wife, Emma, had left when Helen was only two years old. Emma had gone to live in Canada where her family came from, saying it was because she couldn't handle Dad's work hours as a fireman. Dad always had to be away from home a lot. He believed the marriage broke up because Emma had been very young when she married – she'd only been nineteen and Dad was twenty-five. Helen was born two years later, although Emma never seemed to be naturally maternal at that age and agreed to let Helen stay with her Dad when she left for Canada.

So then Dad met Becky eighteen months later and they got married eighteen months after that. They were both the same age, thirty-two. Helen had always called Becky 'Mum' as she was the only real Mum Helen had ever properly known and loved. Helen did receive cards at Christmas and on her birthdays from Emma in Canada, and when she was fourteen, she'd met up with her twice when Emma had come over to London. There was too much ground to make up though, for there to be any kind of proper reunion and Helen loved Holly and George so much she never seriously considered Emma's offer to come and spend time with Emma's new family in Canada.

Helen had been eight when Holly was born and thirteen when George came along nearly five years later. She loved playing with her younger brother and sister even though there was a considerable age gap. In fact she was playful with most people she met. She had a strong mischievous streak and loved to play pranks, traits which Holly and George were fast inheriting as they grew up, often to the exasperation of their parents who had to try and restore the peace. But there was always laughter and happiness in the house and Mum would say they all got on like a house on fire, except this was one fire she never wanted Dad to put out.

Holly didn't climb up in her Poppy Tree quite so often these days, although by coincidence she had climbed up as far as the old magpie nest just last week when she was trying to think what she could write about for a talk she had to do in front of her school tutor group in a few weeks' time.

George had been climbing it more and more recently anyway - he liked to drop his soldiers with homemade napkin parachutes from its branches so it wasn't so easy to find quiet time just for herself any more.

A sudden gust of wind blew through the branches and

reminded her that it was getting chilly, and she thought about going back inside. The sun was quite low over the houses in the distance, and she could see the roof of her school three roads away. Next week will be a mid-term break, a whole week off school, she reflected, and her mind wandered off to what she might do with all that free time.

"Ho-l-l-y!"

She was jolted back to the present as she heard her name being called from somewhere in the garden. "Ho-l-l-y, where are you?" It was George, come to look for her. "Holly, Mum says to come inside and light the candles on the cake."

Holly sighed loudly. She wasn't going to get any peace and quiet after all. Sure enough, looking down, she saw George's little round face peering up at her, and he was starting to climb the tree.

"Mum says she needs you to light the candles in five minutes, so you have to come in," he called up.

Holly was about to say something grumpy, to tell him that she didn't care about cakes, candles or him for that matter, and that she just wanted to be left alone, but she saw George climbing up towards her and she suddenly felt like she should act the proper big sister, like Helen always had been to her. Without saying anything she reached her hand down

14

for him to grab, and he took it and scrambled up alongside her on the branch. Holly held onto his little hand as they sat there and since neither of them really had anything to say, they just sat, hand in hand, in silence, looking out towards the setting sun.

After a few moments Holly looked across at George and saw that his eyes were closed. His little red-cheeked face looked so peaceful, so she thought she would just rest her eyes too, just for a few moments, before going back in to light the candles on Helen's anniversary cake.

CHAPTER 3

Curious Messages

Another gust of wind blew through the branches, scattering the honeysuckle blossom along the gnarled lower branch.

After a little while had passed, Holly was about to suggest that they go back into the house before it got too chilly, but as she looked down she saw something very strange.

"George, look!" she said excitedly. "Look at the branch!"

George looked down to where she was pointing, and he saw it too.

The wind had blown the honeysuckle blossom along the branch, but the petals seemed to form a word. It was unmistakeable. A single, yellow-petalled word:

CLIMB

Holly and George looked at each other and then back at the branch. It was too spooky.

"How did that happen?" wondered George aloud.

Then they both looked up. Were they supposed to climb up higher? They'd both climbed it many times, well, at least as far up as Dad said was safe. Maybe there was another place to climb? Holly was just about to look for another place to climb when she thought she saw...well it looked like...it couldn't be...was that the smiley woman high up in the branches?

It looked like her but it was dusk and the sun had almost set in the distance, so it was possible her eyes were playing tricks and she was just seeing shadows.

"I can see a woman up there!" said George. "It looks like she's smiling at us!"

That clinched it for Holly. Now they had both seen the woman and it was obvious to her what they had to do. "Come on, George, we have to climb higher," she said assertively.

"But the candles!" protested George.

"The candles can wait," replied Holly, already grasping the branch above her head and swinging herself onto her feet. "Come on George, or are you a going to be a Scaredy Chicken Chops all your life!"

"I am *not* chicken..." protested George, who was unsure if climbing higher right now was a very wise thing to start. It would be dark soon, and it was definitely getting colder.

"Zonko!" droned Holly, automatically grimacing back at him over her shoulder. However, she was now on a mission, and she wasn't interested in talking about it any more, or zonking George for that matter. There are times when big sisters just have to lead by example, she thought to herself, and she climbed higher and higher without waiting for George. She was pretty sure he'd follow; he never liked to feel he was being left out of anything.

She was right. On the lower branch George took a last, lingering look at the honeysuckle petals, which were starting to blow off the branch and onto the grass below, then up at his sister who was climbing purposefully upwards. He sighed, blowing his cheeks out, shrugged his shoulders and started to climb up quickly behind her.

Holly didn't look down until she got to the forked branch where the crows had built the original nest over a number of years. It was massive now, since the crows had come back to it for many years and added more twigs to it each time they laid their eggs.

A few years ago the crows had all flown away and some magpies had taken it over. Magpies do that – they borrow things, and then forget to give them back. Coins, jewels, nests - anything really. It's not that they are mean, Helen explained once, it's just that they love to find new things to play with, especially shiny things, and they get so involved so quickly and energetically they find it difficult to remember for very long what they were last up to.

Helen loved magpies. She would always wave at them whenever she saw them, and she made Holly wave too. "Magpies are naughty but fun," she used to say. "They just can't help making mischief around them because otherwise they would get bored easily. It seems like they are always squabbling about something but it's not serious, it's just the way they are…" (Holly had been reminded of a few of her friends at school who behaved just like those magpies but she kept it to herself,) "…you must always wave to them and in return they'll keep you smiling all day!"

Four years ago, on Holly's eighth birthday, the magpie chicks had outgrown the nest and Helen and Holly had watched the whole family fly away. They didn't know it at the time, but the magpies had decided to move on permanently and cause mischief somewhere else. They had never returned and the nest had been empty ever since. The nest was as high as Mum and Dad would let them climb. "That's high enough," Mum would say to her and George, "any higher and you'll be in Heaven before your time."

A little out of breath now, Holly sensed that it would be foolish and probably dangerous to climb much higher because the branches were much thinner and were waving around in the evening breeze. She propped herself up on the thick forked branches next to the nest and thought about everybody back in the warm house and wished she had stayed inside. It was starting to get really chilly now.

And on top of that she was a bit confused too; there was no sign of the smiley woman anywhere. She had done her disappearing act again.

While she waited for George to catch up, Holly reached into her pocket and pulled out another handful of honeysuckle petals and funnelled them slowly through her fist, making a small pile right in the middle of the magpies' nest.

George arrived, puffing his cheeks out and blowing hard. He sat himself next to her, his legs dangling astride the forked branches.

"Where did the woman go?" he asked out loud, but more to himself than to Holly.

Another chilly gust of wind swooshed through the branches.

"I don't get it," said George, "first the petals tell us to climb up here, then we see a woman who disappears, and now we're…"

His voice trailed off as he looked over at his sister. Her face seemed like it was frozen in surprise and shock, her mouth wide open and her eyes fixed on the nest.

"What?" demanded George.

Holly couldn't find any words at first so she just slowly raised her arm and pointed into the middle of the nest.

George peered past her, then twisted his neck to get a look from a different angle. His mouth fell open too.

"The wind blew it… into…" began Holly.

"It looks like it says…" continued George, but he couldn't finish his sentence either.

There, in the middle of the nest, the wind had re-arranged Holly's pile of blossom into a single word.

No, not a word. A name:

HELEN

CHAPTER 4
The Magpies

"**N**ow this is starting to get seriously weirdy," exclaimed Holly. "What else could possibly happen now?"

George was shivering a little next to her, and she put her arm round his shoulders and pulled him closer to her. He put his head on her arm and drew his knees up to his chest to keep warm.

"Maybe it's time to…" Holly began, but George interrupted her.

"Holly! Look up there!"

Two huge, brightly glowing shapes had caught his eye and circled the tree, coming closer and closer. Then three, no…four more behind. As they adjusted their eyes to the dusky sky they could see the shapes were big birds…Owls? Seagulls? Eagles? No, they were enormous magpies, much larger than any magpies they could ever remember seeing. George was becoming quite scared and was nestling up closer under Holly's arm.

"It's OK, Georgie," she whispered, soothingly. "I think they're friendly, that's why they're glowing." She was feeling anxious herself though, but she didn't want George

23

to know. She sat up straight and, thinking of what Helen used to tell her, started to wave at them as they flew down towards the nest.

A few seconds later and the first two had settled next to Holly on the branch. What was happening? Holly wondered. What did they want?

If Holly and George were surprised by huge, glowing magpies landing next to them in the first place, they were astonished when the first one actually spoke.

"Put your feet on the nest, you two," it said in a friendly woman's voice. "Just relax and make yourselves as comfortable as you can. My name is Rilke, and this is Tik," introducing her companion next to her. "And these are our friends, Wakke, Ponke, Teleka and Quok" she continued, waving a wing towards the other four magpies who had landed on the branches just above.

"Wakke - at your service!" The nearest one introduced himself with an exaggerated bow, deliberately poking his diamond-shaped tail into the face of his friend standing on the branch next to him.

"Such a pleasure, an all too rare treat! Ponke, by the way," added another, and gave a little peck to his friend's tail.

"And *I*..." began the third, trying to jostle herself into a position where she could be seen clearly, since the first two had moved in front of her making it difficult for Holly and George to see her, "am Teleka." As she said her name she put her right foot out and pushed Ponke so hard he fell off the branch and landed on a smaller one below, where he was obliged to flap his wings furiously to stop himself from overbalancing.

"And so...you must be...?" asked Holly, pointing at the sixth magpie who seemed content to stay out of the way of his roguish companions.

"Quok" said Quok, quietly.

"Doesn't say much, him," explained Wakke.

"'Cept 'Quok'," cackled Ponke.

"Don't you two start on him now." warned Teleka, lifting her right leg towards the others menacingly.

So many questions came into poor Holly's head. She tried to voice them all at once but all that came out was "But Helen...but Mum..." and then she stopped because she didn't know what the rest of her sentence was going to be. George just clung on tight to his branch.

"Come on, onto the nest," repeated Rilke to Holly and George. Then she turned to the other magpies and chuckled "and that's enough shenanigans from you lot for now."

Holly started to place one foot gingerly onto the nest.

"It's not big enough...strong enough... to hold us," said

George in a small voice, and that was the cue for Tik to speak up. His tone was deeper – a cheerful, kind, man's voice.

"Don't worry about a thing, George old man, it's big enough *and* perfectly strong enough, you'll see. Come on, both feet, both of you, that's the ticket! Now wait for the magic cord and we'll be away!" he called, and he and Rilke hopped down on to the branch next to the nest so that Holly and George could lean against them as they balanced unsteadily on the nest.

"The magic cord…?" began George, and then stopped as he noticed a thin silver thread that seemed to start at his chest and led up towards the sky as far as the fading light allowed him to see. And right in front of him, clinging onto his shoulder with one hand, and onto Rilke's wing with the other, he could see that Holly had one too.

"What is it? Where are we going?" asked Holly.

"Helen wants you to come with us so she can show you her new school!" explained Rilke.

"Helen?? You know my sister??!! But Helen's…in Heaven!" shouted Holly, as the chilly evening wind whistled around her face, almost drowning her words as they came out of her mouth. "She died…she felt dizzy and then… and now… now she's gone to Heaven. At least, I suppose that's

26

where she's gone..." she found herself explaining wistfully to the magpies.

"Of course I know her, my dear, and that's where we're going too, Holly" said Rilke, in a soothing voice. "We'll be there in two tugs of Teleka's talons! Now, hold tight to your magic cords – it's take-off time!" And with that, the two birds picked up one side of the nest each in their claws and flew effortlessly up and out of the tree.

Holly clung with both hands to her flimsy silver thread, as she had been instructed, and miraculously, as she closed her fingers around it, the thread seemed to be as solid as if she had been holding onto a lamp post, despite it being no thicker than George's little finger. She screwed her eyes up tightly against the wind, but after a few seconds, curiosity got the better of her and she opened her left eye a chink, then a bit more and then her right eye till they were both wide open.

"Woweeee!" she shouted at the top of her voice, "Woooohhhhooooooooo! Cooo-oooolll!"

She looked over at George, who had one hand on his cord and the other was gripping her sweater so tightly his knuckles were white. When he heard his sister shouting into the wind he gradually loosened his grip on her sweater, and he too relaxed into this unexpected adventure.

A few minutes later, they had both forgotten their nerves and were loving this magical ride. They heard Rilke, on the right, saying to Tik, "should we?" and Tik replying, "we most certainly should!"

What now? Holly wondered. What were they planning?

"Hold on very tight now!" called Tik, and before they had a chance to ask what was going to happen, it happened. Rilke and Tik banked up sharply, almost vertically and then turned backwards, upside down for a few seconds before plummeting down the other side of an enormous loop-the-loop manoeuvre. Holly and George found themselves clinging on to their cords for dear life, as the two mischievous magpies complimented themselves, cackling merrily all the while.

"Very smooth, Rilke, my dear!" called Tik

"Almost the perfect circle, Tikky!" Rilke called back.

Over the next few minutes, Holly and George enjoyed the most amazing aerobatics they could ever imagine, with Rilke, Tik and their four friends swooping, diving, and rolling, at speeds that took their young passengers' breaths away. It was like a seemingly endless airborne roller-coaster ride and Holly and George adored every second of it.

Finally the aerobatics stopped, and Rilke and Tik concentrated on pulling the nest on a steep incline, shooting up and up. Holly and George were fast losing sight of the houses down below, the cars, the roads and green fields all shrinking as they climbed ever higher. They noticed all the amazing, vivid colours in the sky as they rose above the clouds. The sun warmed their faces once again even though it had been nearly night-time a few moments before in their garden. All at once they were aware that they had both started feeling really happy; as happy, warm and safe as they could ever remember feeling.

Holly's mind was reeling. Where had this feeling of happiness come from? And where were the birds taking them? George was by now just giggling at everything, loving this fantastic ride. It was space travel just as he'd imagined it would be, just like all the games he'd invented with his friends. Only now it was happening for real!

After several minutes of flying, with the birds flapping their strong wings up, up, up above the clouds, Holly noticed that they were slowing down and levelling out.

Tik turned his head slightly over his shoulder and called back to them. "We'll be arriving soon so listen carefully. I want you both to hold hands, close your eyes and count slowly to five. The Soul Council has allowed us to give you Soul Senses until you leave so when you open your eyes again you'll be able to see and hear everything in more or less the same way that we can."

"Who are the Soul Council?" Holly started to ask, more out of nervousness than anything, reaching out to take her brother's hand.

"There's a good time to find out everything important, Holly," chuckled Rilke. "Right now would be a good time for counting!"

Holly took a look at her brother. His eyes were wide open and his cheeks were dimpled and red from laughing, the corners of his mouth set in a permanent smile. She pursed her lips and gave him one of her wide-eyed big sister glares and then squeezed her eyes tight shut. George stuck his tongue out even though he knew she couldn't see him. He was reluctant to shut his eyes but as he saw Holly about to start counting he suddenly thought that whatever it was that they were about to see might not happen if he didn't do as Rilke instructed. He followed his sister's example and closed his eyes too.

"One......two...... " Holly started, too slowly for George's liking.

Hurry up, hurry up! He thought to himself, desperate to take a sneaky-peek while Holly was counting, impatient to find out what Soul Senses would be like. He only just managed to force himself to keep his eyes shut while Holly finished.

"Three......four......five," she finally finished, and George opened his eyes immediately. Holly did too and they both shut them again just as quickly. Double take! What was in front of their eyes was too amazing to understand all in one go. Holly opened her left eye a fraction and peeked through till she could make some sense of the shapes in front of her. Slowly she opened both eyes at once and then blinked several times. All around were brilliant, vivid colours. She felt the same glowing warmth she'd felt earlier while they'd been flying. It seemed to come from inside her stomach and fill her legs and arms and up her neck into her head and then...

Splatch!

Without warning she experienced a blinding flash inside her head right behind her temples and she let out an involuntary sort of "aaaafff!" sound. The same thing must have happened to George because she heard him say something like "yeeeepss!" and when she looked round at him he was rubbing his eyes too, a look of bafflement on his face.

The children realised that they were preparing to land in a marvellous, magical multi-coloured meadow. Vivid scarlet fuschia blended regally in amongst the backdrop of bougainvillea bushes, their orange and violet blossom creating a comforting feeling of safety and happiness. Purple-leaved acers, olive trees, luminous yellow mimosa and lime-green firs framed the corners of the meadow giving way to towering maple and cypress trees behind. A blanket of bluebells and snowdrops stretched away into a small copse of eucalyptus and silver birch.

It was as beautiful a meadow as one could ever imagine. The leaves and blossoms and petals all appeared to have a sort of sunny golden-white haze around them, and Holly noticed that their kaleidoscopic colours seemed almost to be changing depending from which direction she looked at them.

Chaffinches and wagtails darted from one tree to another, and a family of proud jays hopped slowly and importantly across the field of wild grass and daisies, preening their dazzling plumages. Skylarks and blackbirds sang uninhibitedly to each other as pairs of tortoiseshell butterflies flitted amorously in and out of clumps of tall-stemmed black-eyed susans. Everywhere they looked was ablaze with warmth and colour.

As they glided smoothly downwards they circled over an expanse of perfectly manicured gardens, with neatly trimmed laurel bushes interspersed at intervals with scented rosemary and bay trees. Ornamental twisted bonsais and stunted firs bordered paths of fine yellow gravel leading to fountains spouting from meticulously sculpted mythical figurines into ponds filled with sleek Koi carp. In the distance they caught a glimpse of an impressive waterfall to the left of some huge white stone steps leading up to an enormous white palace that stretched towards the horizon as far as their eyes could see.

The palace was bathed mostly in a bright, whitish, purplish, yellowish light. In fact, when they concentrated more closely, its colossal arches, pillars and towers, made of hand-chiselled stone, marble and crystal, seemed to have a little of every imaginable colour about them.

Their attention was distracted by a pervasive scent wafting past their nostrils; familiar smells they both recognised from the grocery store on the corner near their house.

"I can smell Lemon Drops and Peppermint," announced Holly, which were two of her favourite flavours.

George, not to be out-done added "*I* can smell Liquorice All-Sorts," which he adored too.

They would never have believed it if someone had told them that Heaven would smell of their favourite sweets.

All of their senses were being ambushed at once and both

children were so mesmerised they didn't even register that the nest had been brought in to land without the slightest bump by the cheerful magpies. They were jolted out of their daydreams by the sound of Rilke and Tik congratulating themselves on the perfect landing.

"Like a leaf on a millpond, Rilke my sweet," said Tik.

"Smoother still, Tiks," replied Rilke. "A bee on a rose petal more like."

"You have it exactly," agreed Tik, nuzzling his companion's neck affectionately with his beak.

Rilke turned to Holly and George. "Don't be nervous now," she said in a calming voice, "you'll get used to everything in no time at all. Follow me, there's someone who wants to give you a big hug!"

Holly and George were so befuddled that they hadn't noticed that their silver cords had disappeared. They just followed meekly behind Rilke, while Tik and the others stayed in the meadow by the nest, waving their big black and white and green wings at them and cackling softly to each other.

Rilke led them towards a red gate in front of a brick house that looked…exactly like their own house! In fact that gate looked like their own front gate too! So many questions came into their heads all at once that this time all Holly could say was "Where…?" and George managed "But how…?" and since neither one had any idea what the rest of their sentences were likely to be, they both fell silent, standing stock still with their mouths wide open.

CHAPTER 5

Helen

Down the path came a young woman dressed in beautiful white robes with a golden-white glow around her body. As she reached the gate where Holly was standing Holly suddenly knew that it was... but it couldn't be... it was...it was Helen, big sister Helen who had died a year ago! And now here she was again in front of her, in front of the house, their house, and she seemed to walk right through the gate without opening it, right up to where Holly and George were standing.

She was smiling the happiest smile Holly and George had ever seen. It was as if every part of her was smiling; her mouth, her hair, her arms, her feet and even the ground around her seemed to be smiling. Just being next to her made Holly and George smile too, even though Holly had tears streaming down her face at the same time. She noticed her hands were shaking, her shoulders were heaving up and down uncontrollably and her knees felt like they were made of jelly, but there was nothing she could do to stop trembling.

Just as she thought she was going to crumple up in a heap she felt Helen's arms around her waist, Helen's cheek against her cheek and Helen's soothing voice in her ear saying, "Be happy, Hols. Everything is just as it should be. I'm going to show you both the most wonderful, amazing things."

Holly's wet face was squashed up against her sister's cheek, and she could only squint out of the corner of one eye and that was full of tears anyway. But she could make out the red gate and George, standing quiet and hesitant next to it. She became aware of dozens more people all around them watching the three of them with the same all-over-happiness and golden-white glow that Helen had.

She pulled back from Helen a few inches, not wanting to let go of her sister but needing to see her more clearly. She wiped away her tears on her sleeve, and then nestled her head back against Helen's warm cheek. She felt so safe and wanted to stay like that forever.

However, after a few moments, Helen kissed her tears away and held her at arm's length, looking at her through her kind, hazel-brown eyes. Then she turned towards George and he came running into her embrace just as Holly had done, hugging her tightly and clinging on to her robe.

After several moments she pulled back once more, caressing their cheeks with the backs of her out-stretched hands.

"It's so wonderful to see you both again. The Soul Council has allowed you to come and visit Soul School up Here. I asked them if I could help you understand why I had to leave you all down there on Earth last year, and to make it alright for you."

"But our house…" George began.

"Oh, this isn't really our house," Helen explained, gesturing towards the building that Holly and George thought they had recognised, "…or our gate. When someone first arrives up Here we can make them see anything we want them to see just so they feel a bit more at home, but after a while it all disappears into One Big Happiness where we can relax and get ourselves organised."

Organised for what? Holly wanted to ask. And what does One Big Happiness look like? Is this what Heaven looks like? Unfortunately her voice was still not behaving properly so she just stood still while her mouth made lots of silent shapes.

Helen, who seemed to be able to read Holly's mind, replied gently, "You can call it Heaven if you like. Some people call it Heaven, some call it Paradise, or the Garden of Souls. But we Souls just call it Home. You can call it whatever you want, Hols, and don't worry, I'll explain everything in good time. Come on, let's go see the School!"

39

She held out her hands towards Holly and George and they each held one tightly. Then she half skipped and half ran through the meadow where only a few minutes ago they had first landed, pulling her brother and sister breathlessly along with her.

Rilke had rejoined her friends and the entire, mischievous squabble of magpies had re-grouped exactly at the spot where they had arrived in the meadow a few minutes earlier. And, true to form, still all bickering and jouncing with each other, Holly noted with amusement.

"Thank you so much for fetching Holly and George, all of you," said Helen. "It's so wonderful to see them safe and sound up Here."

"Not at all, not at all, a truly blissful ride…"

"The glee is most resoundingly ours, young Helen…"

"Never too much trouble to collect human kinfolk…"

All the magpies replied at once, each bird trying to speak the loudest so that Helen would notice it more than the others.

Except Quok who just quietly said "Quok…"

"You're so kind," said Helen. "Now we must leave you all – we have lots of work to do!"

"Aren't you going to tell them about our Secrets?" Teleka asked, coyly.

"Your Secrets…?" teased Helen, smiling knowingly.

"You know, our secret Magpie Secrets," persisted Wakke, trying to sound mysterious.

"All in good time," laughed Helen. "Come on you two, this way!" And she grabbed their hands and started to run again.

Despite their confusion and their mixed emotions, Holly and George were really excited now. So much was happening all at once. Neither was able to stop the biggest, widest smiles spreading over their faces as they skipped and ran to keep up with Helen.

"That's more like it!" shouted Helen as they ran. "There's only happiness up Here, you'll see!"

" Bup…waj…so…thurb?" spluttered George, running his fastest just to keep up with Helen and making no sense of anything at all. His brain seemed to think the only thing it could do was to invent a new language.

"Here we are!" cried Helen, cheerfully taking no notice of her little brother's puzzled expression. They had arrived in front of the vast marble palace.

"This," she cried theatrically, throwing her arms around in the air, "is Soul School!"

CHAPTER 6
Soul School

Clasping their hands firmly together again, they all drifted up and inside one of the magnificent chambers. It seemed as if they had to just imagine being inside it and there they were inside. Holly could make out the shapes of dozens, no, hundreds of people of all different ages and they seemed to be glowing with all different sorts of colours, just like the magpies had been when they first appeared in the Poppy Tree. But these people were all practically transparent too. George thought it was mind-boggling to be able to see right through them all. He noticed they seemed to just float around from one place to another but yet no one ever collided.

They both looked at Helen with their new Soul Senses and realised now for the first time that Helen too was transparent like all the rest. Everyone seemed to know where they were going, and when they looked more closely they saw that many of them were moving around in pairs. In each pair, one of the people seemed to have a kind of a purple tinge surrounding them.

"First of all, that purpley colour you can see is called indigo," said Helen, who was able to read all the thoughts

43

going on in her brother's and sister's overwhelmed brains. George couldn't remember ever hearing of indigo so Holly told him it was one of the colours in the rainbow, the one between violet and blue and George thought he knew which one it was.

"And second, when we are Home we are not called people any more, we are called Souls," explained Helen. "The Souls you see surrounded by indigo are the Soul Guides, so you'll know how to recognise them from now on. Every Soul that has just arrived Home is paired up with its own Soul Guide. After the Homecoming party is over and the new Soul has settled in a bit, the Guides accompany the new Souls to a classroom to show them all the things that happened to them in their life on Earth. Well, all the important things anyway.

"It's a bit like watching a DVD of our whole life," she continued. "All the good things, all the silly things, all the choices we made, all the mistakes, all the generous things, the special moments and the careless ones. Then we talk about what we learned from that life, whether we felt we achieved what we were supposed to achieve, and then we can go and relax for a little while, and have some fun while we get used to being Home again."

"Have you seen your DVD? Can I see it? Am I in it?" blurted out Holly, who was suddenly overcome with dozens of questions, and this time the words came tumbling out. "How did the Souls know what they were supposed to do in the first place? And do they get told off if they did a lot of naughty things? And why are some of them really old when they die and you were so young? Why did you have to die anyway? I don't want you to be up Here, I want you to come back home again! Proper home, I mean, our home. And…"

So many thoughts and questions were coming out of Holly's brain that her mouth was finding it hard to keep up, and she found that tears were welling up in her eyes again. Helen was still smiling that special, affectionate, big sister smile. Despite her tears Holly felt safe and calm once more. More questions kept spilling out of her mouth and Helen patiently waited for Holly's tears and questions to stop. Holly suddenly felt very sheepish so she turned and hugged Helen as tightly as she could, not wanting to show the tears that were still trickling down her cheeks, and not wanting to ever let go in case her sister disappeared again.

After a few minutes Helen sat down on the ground and pulled Holly down next to her. She shushed her sobs with one finger against Holly's lips and wiped her tears lovingly away with her soft fingertips.

"It's natural that you have so many questions," said Helen. "It's difficult for people to give satisfying answers when someone dies young. I've been given permission to show you what it's like here in Soul School and answer your questions as best I can. Then you'll understand what happens to us Souls when our human body dies. And most of all I want to show you that it's OK to be happy when you go back to Earth again."

"But you look so happy, and so...well, so normal up Here!" Holly said in a half-whisper.

"I know, Hols," agreed Helen patiently. "Let me try and explain. I'll start with when we die, OK? 'Cos that's the beginning of everything really..."

"You mean the end, don't you...?" asked Holly, frowning.

"No, Super Sis, I mean the beginning – you'll see what I mean in a bit. It's the end for the physical body, it's true. You could say a Soul just *wears* its human body, like a human wears its clothes. And bodies, like clothes come in all sorts of colours, sizes, and designs. After a time when they are old and no use any more we throw them away and choose new ones. Dying just means we throw our physical bodies away - sometimes we bury them and sometimes we cremate them..."

"Like your body was..." interrupted George, remembering the funeral.

46

"That's right, Georgie. Mum and Dad decided to cremate my physical body and scatter the ashes around the big old tree in the garden where we all loved to play..."

"Around my Poppy Tree?? I never knew that!" Holly interrupted, a bit louder than she had intended.

"Nor me," said George solemnly.

"I know, they decided not to tell you in case you felt strange about playing there afterwards," explained Helen. "They knew how much you both love playing in that tree and they thought it might upset you."

"It wouldn't upset me," said George. "I think it would make me play there more, knowing that you were...well... kind of...there with me."

"Me too," agreed Holly. "Now I know why I always feel happy in it, because it's got you, sort of... sprinkled all around it."

"Oh, I love you both so much!" cried Helen. "You are both so special to be able to accept and understand things like this. Now where was I? Oh yes, so the physical body is buried or cremated on Earth, and in the meantime our Soul body comes back Home. Up Here I mean. Like I said, we call this place Home.

"When our Soul body is freed from the physical body, it's also freed from all the illnesses and disabilities and restrictions that our physical bodies might have experienced on Earth," she continued.

"Then shouldn't everyone up Here, I mean every *Soul* up Here, look the same as every other Soul?" Holly asked.

"That's a good question, Hols, and I know why you're asking it. The answer is they all *do* look identical…"

"No they don't!" George burst in, "I can see old people…I mean *Souls*, old Souls, young Souls, big Souls, little Souls, all with different coloured skins, different faces - they're all different, just like on Earth!"

"Yes, I know that's what they look like to you both," said Helen smiling. "I was going on to say - before you interrupted me, Georgie Porge - they all look identical to *us* up Here. Remember, the Soul Council has given you special Soul Senses so you can see and hear *more or less* what we all see up Here. All these Souls you're seeing are allowing you to see and hear them *more or less* as you might imagine they looked on earth. This way, the things you see up Here will fit more easily with what your minds are expecting and you can make sense of it a lot better."

"I want to see what you see," objected George. "I want to see what Souls really look like!"

"And hear what they hear too," added Holly, a little self-consciously, because she thought it might be a little scary in reality.

"I thought you might say that!" laughed Helen. "Well the truth is there's not much to see really because all we have become is just a form of light. And hearing us could be…well, let's just say a little complicated…"

"Can you let us? Please, Helen. Just for a short while. Just so we know what it feels like… Please…" George was difficult to rein in when he started begging insistently like this and Helen relented happily.

"OK, Mister, you asked for it! You too, Hols?"

Holly nodded, shakily.

"Right, close your eyes while I count to five…and no sneaky-peeks either! "Onetwothreefourfive!" she counted quickly.

Splatch! That blinding flash occurred behind both their temples again, only a little more intensely this time it seemed.

"Oooouppffffhhh!"

"Aaammmmmmmhh!"

"Open wide!"

Both of them opened their eyes and adjusted their vision, but there was nothing to be seen really. Everywhere was a brilliant glow of all different colours, swirling around in every direction. Helen was no longer anywhere to be seen either, she had dissolved into the shimmering typhoon of light.

But it was the noise that was the most difficult to adjust to. It was as if hundreds of voices were all chattering at once, and Holly and George were obliged to listen to all of them. Even when they covered their ears, it was as if the voices were already inside their heads. Holly remembered that Helen had warned them it would be deafening, and it certainly was.

After a few minutes of this crazy torrent of words, colours, lights and thoughts, an over-riding voice came into both their heads simultaneously, and they recognised it as Helen's. "Seen and heard enough?" the voice teased gently, and both of them gasped "Yes!"

"Get ready then!" Another quick flash arrived, which they were both expecting this time, so it didn't catch them unawares, and then they were back with their previous Soul Senses.

"So... how was that, then?" Helen asked brightly.

"Coo-oolll!" cried George, although his sisters suspected a little bravado on his part as he was looking quite flustered. "It was like when we stood under that big waterfall in the Water Park and you couldn't really see or hear anything, or even really think about anything with all the water smashing down on your head!"

Holly actually agreed that that was a pretty good description of exactly what it had felt like, and she was still feeling a little shaky herself.

"We'll stay down at this level of Soul Senses, shall we then?" Helen giggled. "So now you've got a glimpse of how Souls can move around at incredible speeds, in several different directions at the same time and communicate with hundreds of Souls and people at once, and read minds and see into the future."

"Just like Superman can!" said George. "And Santa Claus aswell, prob'ly. 'Cept everyone knows only Santa Claus is real, 'cos Superman's powers are just comic-pretend, aren't they?" he stated authoritatively.

Helen glanced over at Holly and they smiled to each other.

CHAPTER 7

Good Grief

Helen resumed her explanation. "You can see everyone is looked after up Here so you don't have to worry that we are unhappy or lonely. Everyone has their own Guide to take care of them and to teach them and I have so many friends and loved ones up Here that I haven't seen for ages. I'm having so much fun!"

"But I miss you!" cried Holly. "And Mum misses you, and Dad too. We all want you to come back!"

"I know you do. But just because we die doesn't mean everyone has to feel sad – just the opposite in fact! And that's exactly why the Soul Council has allowed you to visit us up Here. So you can understand how to miss us in a happy and a positive way! Grief is a natural experience for all humans…"

"What does 'Grief' mean?" asked George.

"Grief means living your life in a different way from before because you're missing someone who's left you or who's died," explained Helen. "And living life in that different way is called grieving. People grieve in many different ways."

"You mean when they become unhappy and depressed,

and say nasty things to other people?" asked Holly.

"Well, they can behave like that sometimes, although they often don't really mean to be nasty," agreed Helen, "and…"

"Sometimes even Dad gets a bit angry," interrupted George.

"Anger can be part of grief too," Helen admitted. "In fact, humans can react in many different ways when a loved one dies or leaves the family unexpectedly. There are negative reactions but there can be positive reactions too. On the negative side, people can become unhappy or depressed or nasty or angry, as you say. Or they can become violent or withdrawn or just feel like they have no energy to do anything so people call them lazy.

"Sometimes they spend the rest of their lives blaming *themselves* for the person's death and punish themselves, believing *they* were the reason, or even that *they* don't have any right to be happy ever again. Sometimes they think it's not even worth *themselves* living any longer and they start to do dangerous or risky things."

"So grief is a really bad thing, then?" George was concentrating intensely.

"No, Georgie, not at all. Like I said, by itself, grief just means living in a *different* way, not necessarily a bad or a good way. *Bad* grief, like some of the things I just talked about, is not often very productive. *Good* grief however, can be a really rewarding and enriching experience."

"So what exactly do you mean by '*good grief*,' then?" Holly wanted to know.

"Good grief is when people react in a really positive way, even though they still miss the person who's died," explained Helen, patiently. "Let me try to give you an example," she offered. "Missing someone who has died is a very special feeling because it brings to the surface all the love you have for that someone. And that someone's Soul still loves everyone it has left behind on Earth too, just as much as before, even though it's no longer there *in person*.

"Every time someone misses us because we've gone from Earth, or sends a little prayer, that message is sent to us immediately. You've talked to me and thought about me many times since I died last year, haven't you?"

Holly and George both nodded.

"Up Here those rays of bright lights you see above you everywhere are what prayers and special thoughts, to and from Earth, look like." Helen continued. "Look up all around you! You're going to notice them zapping around all over the place now you have Soul Senses."

Holly and George both looked up, and sure enough, now that Helen had made them aware, they both noticed the hundreds and thousands, millions probably, of light beams of all different colours, streaming across the horizon in every direction, at supersonic speeds.

"Many people think that when someone dies there's no way of contacting them any more and it makes them sad," Helen told them. "It's just not true as you can see..." she waved her hand at the thought-beams that lit up the sky. "But because they believe that though, it makes them feel really alone and helpless too, and they busy themselves doing a million and one things to take their mind *off* missing their loved one..."

"...when what they could be doing is the opposite?" Holly was cottoning on.

"That's one way to look at it," agreed her sister. "When you put your minds *on* your loved one, those thought-rays find their way to the right Soul every time without fail, you can be sure of that. Then we send light-beam messages back to you to help you do something special while you are thinking of us."

"So then people wouldn't feel like doing so many negative things either, would they?" George chimed in solemnly.

"Absolutely right, Georgie!"

"Can we talk to our own Soul too, or does it have to be

the Soul of the person who's died?" Holly wanted to know.

"Every Soul knows everything there is to know in the whole Universe, Holly. So it doesn't matter really which Soul you seek out for answers, they will all tell you what you need to know."

"But our own Soul is the closest so will the answers come quickest from there?" asked George.

"Your own Soul is always a good place to start, especially if you're in a hurry to know something," smiled Helen.

"So, when you do something really special while you're thinking about the person you're missing, is that positive griefing?" George thought he understood.

"Positive *grieving*," Helen gently corrected his pronunciation. "Yes, that's exactly what it is. So next time you miss me, think of something to ask me and I can send you an answer straight from Soul School. That way you can do wonderful things every time you think about me."

"But I think about you all the time!" pouted Holly, her bottom lip sticking out in front of her and quivering a little.

"So just think of how many fabulous things you'll be able to do!" laughed Helen pushing Holly's lip back with her forefinger so it was level with her top lip, where it belonged. "Right, that's enough of all that for now. Come on, see that wonderful Hall over there? That's the Library, let's go and have a look and you can ask me questions on the way!"

CHAPTER 8

Seven For A Secret

"Helen…?" George piped up a few seconds later.

"Mmm?"

"Is that the one of the secrets, then?"

"Is *what* one of *which* secrets?"

"You know - the secrets the magpies were talking about."

"Ah. Right. Err…is *what* a secret the magpies were talking about?"

"If we…I mean, *when* we miss you, we just have to send you a thought message and you will send us back messages about good things to do…?"

"If I told you, they wouldn't be secrets any more, would they, Clever Trevor!"

Holly's curiosity got the better of her. "Yes, but they asked you if you were you going to tell us their secret Magpie Secrets, not just any old secrets," she reasoned, "so why would they say that if they didn't want us to know them?"

"Yes, and you said 'all in good time' too," added George. "So this is a good time, right now!" He folded his arms meaningfully.

"I can see you two aren't going to let up on this one,"

smiled Helen. "OK, here's what I'll do. I'll explain a little about magpies first, shall I? Magpies, as you have probably noticed, love to be the centre of attention. Everything they do is to get noticed. There is a little rhyme that magpies made up long ago, that you probably know – it starts 'One for Sorrow, Two for Joy…' "

"I know it!" cried George.

"Everyone knows that rhyme," said Holly, "Three for a Girl and Four for a Boy…"

"Five for Silver, Six for Gold…" sang George, out of tune, and all three finished off together, "Seven for a Secret, *never* to be told!"

"That's it, exactly," said Helen. "The original version that the magpies made up was "Seven for *our Secrets*, never to be told,' because they want people to think that the world happens because of them. So when you see one magpie, you might think that it's sad to be all by itself, which might make you think of something sad too, so you look around for a second one so you can think of happy things again…"

"I don't need to see magpies before I can think about happy things," countered Holly, "or sad things or girls or boys…or anything at all, come to that."

"Of course you don't," agreed Helen, patiently. "But magpies like to think you do – that's what makes them feel happy, important – it's just how they are."

"So we met six magpies today, all at once – does that mean we should be thinking about gold?" asked George, logically.

"If you like," replied Helen evenly. "Or you can think about all six things at once, or something completely different – it's up to you."

"So if we saw a seventh magpie, then they would be trying to make us think of a secret?" asked Holly.

"A secret never to be told?" asked George.

"Now that's the fun part," replied Helen. "You see, magpies hardly ever let themselves be seen in groups of exactly seven, because they like to keep that air of mystery about themselves. You might see more than seven together, and usually less - they are such squabblers that the smaller the group the better." She smiled. "And yes," she added mysteriously, lowering her voice to a furtive whisper. "There *might be* a few secrets which you *might* remember while you are up here, but I can't *tell* you what they are – you'll have to see if you can work them out again."

"What do you mean, '*remember*' and 'work them out *again*'?" demanded Holly. "You mean we know them already? I don't understand! Just TELL US!" she wailed, very frustrated now.

"See what a state those mischievous magpies have got you into! That's what they do best, and they are so good at it! Remember we said your Soul knows everything there is to know about everything? Well, think about it. Wouldn't that include all the secrets there are to know too?"

"But a secret is something that someone knows and someone else doesn't," said Holly. "So if everyone knows everything already, then there can't be any secrets can there?"

"I didn't say everyone knows everything, I said '*Souls* know everything.' So…?"

"So there can't be any secrets for Souls, but there can be for humans? I don't understand, I'm confused!" complained Holly.

"The magpies would be cackling so hard if they could see this. Change of subject – ask me a different question," laughed Helen.

Holly and George fell silent for a few moments, trying to make sense of everything, without much success.

"OK, I've got one," said Holly after a pause as she calmed herself down, determined not to allow a bunch of magpies to dictate her mood.

"Ask away!" invited Helen, as the three of them floated slowly across the beautiful lawns towards the Library.

"You said something about a Homecoming – what is that exactly, and what happens?"

"Fab question, Hols! When we first come back Home, you know, up Here, it's called a Homecoming. Simple isn't it!" she beamed at Holly as they neared the magnificent stone and marble building.

"That's it??" asked Holly, disappointed.

"Just teasing, Holly Bolly," Helen winked at George, who grinned up at her. "No, what happens when someone is coming Home is that all the Souls who knew the Homecoming Soul are alerted with a special message. Word gets around up Here in a flash…"

"Literally!" called out George, pointing at the skies.

Helen ruffled his hair affectionately and continued, "…exactly! You've seen the way messages flash around, haven't you! So…dozens of Souls of people that we have known when we were alive on Earth all turn up to our Homecoming to welcome us back. It's thrilling to see each other again. A Homecoming is just like a huge party. I've met Grandma Margot and Great Grandma Millie and so many Souls of people I knew in previous lives too. If someone arrives while you're up Here I'll take you to watch their Homecoming and you'll see what a happy occasion it can be!"

"But…" started George, unsure if the question that had popped up in his mind was very polite, "suppose they weren't ready to…you know, didn't want to leave Earth? I mean, it's cool up Here and everything, but I don't want to leave all my friends, or Mum and Dad, or… you know…yet…" he trailed off.

"…or your gorgeous, clever big sister, don't forget, Dodo Wits!" threw in Holly indignantly, punching his arm.

"My Shaggy-Haired Ostrich-Bellied Blimp sister, you mean," replied George automatically, and then, realizing that zonking probably wasn't very appropriate for Heaven, turned towards Helen sheepishly.

"Er, sorry…" he began, but didn't get any further with his apology because Holly had immediately knelt down next to him and launched a two-handed tickle attack right under his ribcage. He landed flat on his back, curling up in a ball like a hedgehog to avoid her poking fingers.

Tickling always made him scream, and curiously, he could never work out if he liked it or not. Whether it was the pleasure or the discomfort or both together he had no idea. What he did know was that he was completely helpless for as long as someone was tickling him. Even though he wriggled as hard as he could to get away, he hardly ever managed it till the tickler decided to let him go.

Holly taunted him, her mouth shaping each syllable exaggeratedly just two inches from his face, her fingers poking and tickling his ribs mercilessly in rhythm with her words. "No-zon-king-in-Hea-ven-Bo-ney-Boy!"

It was driving George almost out of control and instinctively he managed to stick his tongue full out and treat his sister to a long, slimy lick, starting right under her nostrils and up to the bridge of her nose.

"Eeuugghh! Yuk!" You are so disgusting!" she shouted, outraged but grinning all the same and pulling away to wipe her face on her sweater sleeve. "Did you see what he did?" she asked Helen, as George rolled away and jumped to his feet. "I am *so* going to make you pay for that!"

She sprang to her feet too and started to chase after George, who had moved just out of range, ready to sprint off, away from danger. In an instant Helen had grabbed hold of both her sister's wrists tightly. She started to spin herself round and round, shuffling her feet faster and faster in a circle on the spot. After half a turn Holly's feet left the ground as Helen whirled her round and round, lifting and lowering her in the air like a human Chair-O-Plane.

When she finally brought her back to a standstill, Holly was so dizzy she could hardly stand upright for a few seconds.

"Do it to me, do it to me!" cried George, and Helen, still laughing, grabbed his thin wrists and whirled him round and round and up and down too. She let him down gently too and he made both his sisters laugh as they watched him showing off, staggering around exaggeratedly before finally collapsing on the ground on his back, his arms and legs spread out - a skinny, sweaty, panting heap of happiness and smiles.

The tickling and licking were forgotten already, and Helen took Holly's hand and led her over to where George was lying, and they both lay down either side of George like three sardines in a tin. No-one spoke for a few minutes, all three collecting their own thoughts, gazing upwards at the splendid spectacle in the skies, multicoloured message rays whizzing in every direction.

Helen broke the silence. Propping herself up on her elbows, she smiled at her brother and sister, her eyes shining.

"Right, back to work you two!" she announced, standing up and turning to offer her hands to the others to pull them to their feet too.

"Bossy Baboon!" George chirped under his breath, but it didn't escape Helen, and made her giggle again. She grabbed his neck playfully under her arm and dragged him along a few paces, messing up his hair with her free hand before letting him go.

"So, Mister Memory Man, what did you ask me before we got sidetracked with zonking and tickling?" Helen asked George.

"Ummm...Can't remember," admitted George.

"I can," said Holly. "He asked what happens when people leave Earth who don't want to?"

"That's it, well remembered!" Helen said. "Well it can be tricky sometimes it's true, because some Souls are very upset and confused about leaving Earth, especially if the death happened very suddenly or with little warning. On the other hand, if a human body is ill for some time before it dies, its Soul can get months or even years to prepare properly for its Homecoming. Then it's not confused or upset at all when it comes back Home."

"You...went...well, died I mean, with no warning at all," said Holly, "but you don't seem very confused or upset."

"That's true, I did," smiled Helen. "And in fact I *was* confused up Here for just a little while because I left Earth very suddenly. It did take me a couple of weeks with my Guide to remember exactly the details of the Life-path I chose last time I was up Here. My life with you all, I mean. Shall I tell you what happened immediately after my

Homecoming?"

Her brother and sister nodded, wide-eyed.

"We go first into the Temple of Healing where we go through a sort of shower, only it's not water that showers us, it's light. A kind of healing, cleansing light. All the human emotions that aren't useful to us any more, all the confusion and upset, just gradually washes away and is replaced over time by a sort of loving energy, although we still remember everything about our life on Earth. That way once we start working through our Life Lessons in this Library," Helen waved an arm up at the gigantic building in front of them, "we are relaxed and ready to make sense of everything that we did on Earth."

"When you say Life Lessons, do you mean those 'life DVDs' we talked about?" asked George.

"The very same," said Helen. "I finished working with my Guide on my 'DVD' a few months ago. So when I feel I'm ready I can start choosing my next lessons in the other Library. And after that I can decide on the best pathway to experiencing them back on Earth again."

Holly and George spent the next half an hour asking all the many questions they could think of about Homecomings, previous lives, long-lost relatives, Guides, Life Lessons, DVDs... There just seemed to be a whirlwind of new information to take in all at once. Eventually their questions dried up and Helen decided to divert their attentions.

"Come on," she said, "let me show you something you're going to love!"

CHAPTER 9
Life Lessons

Clasping their hands once more, and again, without seeming to actually walk anywhere, Holly and George found themselves inside the enormous Hall. It hadn't seemed as large from the outside, but now they were inside it seemed vast, with hundreds, no thousands, no…millions, no…*trillions* of books. They stretched into the distance in every direction.

Small books, large books, thick books and thin books and when they looked closer Holly and George could see that the writing on the covers was in all kinds of different languages too. What was really strange, though, was that it seemed to them that they could understand all the foreign words anyway.

Still holding their hands in her own, Helen floated them all up to a high corridor filled with Red Books. Above and below them, were hundreds more corridors and passages and every one was choc-a-bloc full with Red Books.

"These look like books to you although here they are known as Life Lessons," Helen explained quietly. She had lowered her voice because it was a Library after all, and lots of other Souls were studying in silence all around them.

"Every Life Lesson in this Hall contains records of every human Life-path every Soul has ever followed on Earth," she continued.

"Wowwww!" Holly and George mouthed at each other, trying to take in this incredible fact.

"What colour do the books look to you in this Hall?" asked Helen, jauntily, aware of their amazement.

"Red," said George, and Helen nodded.

"They don't look red to us, but it's just so you can see a difference between this Hall and the next one I'll show you later," she explained. "Every time we come back Home, our last Life-path on Earth is reviewed with a Guide. Then the most important things we learned are written into our very own Red Book. As Souls we all have our own Red Book that lets us see how our learning is coming along. "

"Can you read other Souls' Red Books?" asked George, always inquisitive.

"George! You're so nosey, it's not that kind of library," scolded Holly, and then realised that just maybe she might have been a little hasty since she didn't actually *know* if that were true. "Umm...is it, Helen?" she asked a little more softly now, because she suddenly caught herself hoping George would be proved right.

"Yes it is, Hols, and yes we can, George," said Helen

diplomatically. "Any Souls can read any other Souls' Red Books – our Guides help us to find the Life Lessons of other Souls who are travelling along similar Life-paths. That way everyone can learn from everyone else."

George triumphantly put his two thumbs under his nostrils and waved his fingers at Holly, like two deer antlers, pulling an alarmingly ugly grimace towards his sister.

Holly did her best to ignore him as her brain was seriously struggling with all this information, and little snippets were just starting to fall into place.

She turned her back dramatically on George, and looked up at her sister. "Are you telling me…that we have had a life before? I mean, that we've been to Earth once already…and been someone else…in a *previous* life?" she finally managed to ask.

"That's exactly right, my cleverest sister!" smiled Helen. "And not just once, you've been there lots of times and been lots of people!"

"I can't believe that!" cried Holly. "Imagine if I told that to my friends, they wouldn't believe it either. They'd laugh at me."

Helen nodded patiently. "It's not important for the moment whether you, or they, *believe* in having several lives or not, Hols," she explained. "Do you think *I'm* real? Here we are together again, and I died a year ago!"

"Well you *seem* real enough up Here, and up Here *seems* real enough," replied Holly, looking around her. "But this could all be a dream couldn't it? I mean, if it is, and I wake up and find this place doesn't exist, and you're not real again, then there's nothing to believe in, is there?"

"I know it's a difficult idea for you to grasp, because when we are humans, we are programmed to search for proof and experience of things *before* we can believe in them. Souls are programmed simply to *know* things, long before we have experience of them. That's one reason we come to Earth – to *experience* what we already know. So for now, don't worry about believing it or not believing it, see if you can find an answer to questions like: "What if it were true? Would you live this life differently if you knew you were going to get to live another one later? And if so…how?"

"Well," began Holly, who had never considered such questions before, "I s'pose I…well…that is… I…" but too many thoughts and questions popped into her head all at once and she faltered.

"You see," said Helen, patiently. "That's my point. Tricky, isn't it! Suppose believing actually came *first*, and proof *second*, rather than the other way round? How might life be then for people?"

Holly remained pensive.

George wondered if this might be one of the magpies' secrets; he definitely couldn't remember knowing this piece of information before. "So who programmes humans?" he heard himself asking. "Have I been programmed?"

"Yes you most certainly have, Georgie, and *you* programmed *yourself*!" his sister told him. He pulled an 'I'm-completely-baffled-now' sort of face at her.

"I know, I know…" she continued hurriedly, smiling tenderly. "There's a lot to understand, don't worry if it doesn't make sense at first. There's no rush, you'll piece it all together bit by bit I promise. Now, back to business. Take a look around you. Pick a book, any book, and you'll start to understand what happens!"

Holly looked around and pointed to a tall, thin book just above her head.

"OK let's see," said Helen and pulled the book off the shelf and laid it on the table in front of them. Then she started to lift the thick, dusty cover. Holly thought it was hilarious that there was dust in Heaven. She heard Helen chuckling behind her – of course, she could read minds! Holly thought she had better be more careful what she thought about in future, but Helen read that thought too and chuckled even louder. Holly decided she just couldn't win and so, seeing the funny side, she started giggling too.

"What's so funny?" demanded George, who hated being left out of things.

"You two are so adorable!" was all Helen would reply, and kissed them both on the top of their heads. Then she lifted the Red Book cover wide open.

Holly and George were instantly intrigued. There were no pages inside the book, instead a brilliant light shone out and upwards towards the ceiling. "Put your hands in the light," instructed Helen, and Holly and George placed her hands where Helen showed them.

What happened next was really fun. They heard several different voices talking to them, except this time the voices came through one at a time, not like when Helen had briefly allowed them purè Soul Senses. There were all sorts of different voices – some seeming older, some younger, some men's, some girls', women's, boys' - many were even in different languages but once again, somehow Holly and George could understand them perfectly while their hands were in the light. All the voices spoke about events that had happened to them in different circumstances, towns, countries and even in different centuries.

Holly didn't know very much about history, but she loved listening to all these wonderful stories. George was entranced too. They were both captivated as they listened to all sorts of tales… about making friends, about being poor, about fighting, about being loved, about having beautiful clothes, about being famous, about being cruel, about war, about looking after children, about being sad, about winning races, about illness, about…well about so many events. They listened, fascinated, to all the remarkable narratives that were pouring out of the light, through their hands and into their minds.

And at the end of every story what Holly found the most interesting was that the voices talked about what they had *learned and understood* from experiencing those events. And about how they would do things a little differently next time, (*next time* - that phrase again!) because of what they had learned.

"So many people! So many stories!" cried Holly a bit too loudly, and Helen had to put her finger on her lips to remind her that other Souls were studying all around them. "And so many lessons to learn," she added very quietly, glancing round to see if she had disturbed any of them.

"But… Helen?" began George, a little unsure of what he was going to say next. "Well, you know you said everyone has their very own Red Book?"

Helen nodded encouragingly.

"So all those people, all those stories and lessons, they all happened in different lives, at different times," continued George, "but ...because they're all in *just one book*, ...does that mean that... they all *happened to just one Soul?!*"

"Genius Georgie!" grinned Helen. "You're spot on so far! So why do you suppose one Soul might need to have lots of different lives?" she challenged him.

"Because," chipped in Holly, who wanted to show that she had understood it too, "a Soul has to have as many different experiences on Earth as it can, so it can learn as many lessons as it can. So that's why it would have to have many, many different lives too."

"I was going to say that first, if you'd let me," grumbled George.

"Two geniuses in one family!" exclaimed Helen, "you've understood everything there is to understand from this Library in one go! How amazing is that?!"

Both Holly and George beamed at their older sister; she was always so good at making them feel really special with her compliments. Competitive as ever, each one was secretly scanning their brain for another insightful thing to say to get the next compliment all to themselves. Neither spoke for a few seconds and in the end George could only come up with a question.

"What was it like when you saw your own DVD, like…this time?" he asked tentatively. "I mean, your life with me and Holly, and Mum and Dad? Can you show us?"

"I wondered when you might ask me that question," replied Helen. A little note of seriousness had crept into her voice. "I'm afraid that's one 'DVD' I'm not allowed to show you, until you come up Here as proper Souls. That's because we are in the same Soul family you see. My lessons are completely mixed in with you two and with your own lessons. You will have to go back to Earth soon, so it's important that you both follow your Life-paths without my *experiences* influencing your decisions. But I can tell you what it *feels* like to revisit my whole life again if you like. And you can spend as long as you want looking in all the other books too."

Both Holly and George nodded excitedly at the thought of 'reading' more amazing stories and adventures from the Red Books.

"What does it feel like then, to watch your whole life all over again?" asked Holly, excitedly.

"Let me see now, how best can I describe it to you?" pondered Helen. "Well, do you remember when we all went camping about two years ago in the summer?"

Holly and George both nodded.

"You would have been about five, Georgie, and Hols was ten. There was a little stream at the bottom of the camping site, and we spent a whole morning gathering rocks and bits of wood to make a dam."

"And we put those two big boulders in the middle and stacked the wood against it, with all the smaller rocks filling in the gaps, I remember now!" cried George breathlessly. "And all the water stored up behind it and made a little swimming pool and we swam around in it!"

"Yes, and then when we had to go back for lunch-time, Dad made us push the big boulders out and the water burst through so hard it swept away all the stones and wood with it," added Holly. "And George got swept away too, didn't you, Georgie Worgie!" she teased in an impish voice.

"Did not!" lied George, remembering again how scared he'd been as the water had whooshed him at great speed several yards downstream.

"Did too, just like a drowning monkey! And Dad had to wade in, in his jeans and shoes and fish you out!" Holly was enjoying the memory.

"Well, think about it," Helen continued. "Imagine that the swimming pool building up behind the dam is all my memories and experiences and thoughts over my whole life. And then my Guide surrounded me with a bright, golden-white light, and it was just like the dam bursting, and all my memories and experiences and thoughts pouring out in front of me, for me to look at and revisit and discuss."

"Coo-oo-ool!" said George, who was getting desperate to open some more Red Books. "So now where is the Soul whose book we're reading?" he asked.

"That's not important, Georgie," replied Helen. "All I know is that when that Soul returns up Here next time from whatever Life-path it chose last time, it will add its new stories and lessons to this very book. If it has learned the lessons it was supposed to learn from its last Life-path, it can choose which lessons it wants to learn next time."

"Suppose it didn't learn very much?" asked Holly, fascinated.

"Then it chooses a Life-path with similar lessons to learn next time," Helen answered.

"Suppose it liked its life so much last time it wants to do the same sorts of things all over again?" asked George.

"Then it can do that too, as often as it wants, only with different people naturally," replied his sister.

"So, you're telling me that up Here in Soul School *we get to choose the life we want to learn from*?" asked Holly excitedly. Her mind started whizzing round all the things she'd like to choose to have in her own life.

"That's it exactly," confirmed Helen, smiling. Holly couldn't resist a quick, smug, sideways glance at George to see if he was impressed too.

"Freaky! So you could choose to be my sister again, and come back to Earth, except I would be older than you, so you can learn what it's like to be my little sister this time!" giggled Holly. She thought that was a very funny idea. George was laughing too at the thought of Helen as a baby in their house.

"Not so loud, Megaphone Mouth!" shushed Helen, putting her finger to her lips once more.

"So when I choose my new life, is that when I programme myself?" asked George, more quietly this time.

"Well, that's the start of the programming," replied Helen, "but let's not get ahead of ourselves – there's so much more to show you yet!"

"OK, OK so can we open some more Red Books now?" asked George, trying his best not to sound too impatient, although he was bursting with curiosity.

"You can open as many as you like!" allowed Helen. "However, there are three rules. Number one: you may only have one book open at a time; two: you must put all books back exactly where you got them from and three: if a book won't let you open it, it's probably because that Soul's story might be linked in some way to yours, so just choose another, OK?"

Holly and George didn't need a second invitation. They set about exploring corridor after corridor, shelf after shelf, book after book. It was fabulous just thinking about where they wanted to get to and then just magically being there, they didn't have to actually walk anywhere. They heard hundreds and hundreds of stories. Happy stories, sad stories, cruel stories, exotic stories, brave stories, inspiring stories, and dozens of normal, everyday stories.

Helen showed them the most mind-boggling trick so far: by leaning over and putting their faces in the light, they could actually transport themselves *into the stories*. Time and time again, George and Holly transported themselves into different situations and events where they would find themselves standing unseen alongside the characters, seeing what they saw, hearing what they said, and most amazing of all, knowing what they were all thinking and feeling. The stories were unfolding all around them, and they could just observe everything, without anyone in the story knowing they were there.

After a while, Helen decided that that was enough for the

time being. She sent them both a thought message simultaneously: "*I'll make this book my last one for now and go and see what the others are doing.*"

It had the desired effect. Sure enough both Holly and George both reappeared a few minutes later, their faces flushed with the excitement of their first real taste of Soul School.

"Come on both of you, let's go and visit a Soul study class. You can actually meet some Souls who have been working on their own Life Lessons if you want."

"Coo-oooll!" enthused Holly.

George didn't say anything because he suddenly felt a bit shy and he squeezed Helen's hand tightly.

"Don't be shy, Gorgeous Georgus," said Helen soothingly, reading his thoughts. "All the Souls will know exactly what you are thinking and they will answer all the questions you have, probably without you even having to say them out loud. You can do it too with your Soul Senses. Come on, you'll be ace!"

CHAPTER 10
Studying Souls

A few seconds later they found that they had both floated out of the Library and back into a large classroom. Holly counted eighteen desks and chairs all arranged in a horseshoe shape. Five Souls were seated at desks facing in towards the middle and each had a Red Book open in front of them. They all had their hands placed in the bright lights that were shining out, just as they had in the Library. Floating nearby each Soul was a Guide, an indigo glow around each one.

"You see, the Guides are working through the Life Lesson books with their Soul student." Helen was 'thought-speaking' to Holly and George since they were getting used to it now, and she didn't want to interrupt the lessons. "When we first arrive we view the whole book in one sitting so we can get an overall impression of how we behaved in our Life-path on Earth. That gives us a general idea of whether we are pleased or not with what we did and what we learned. Then, when it's had time to sink in, we review little bits at a time, discuss them with our Guide and move on to another bit. That's what these Souls are doing now. Then they will go into R and D groups and share their learning with each other"

"What are R and D groups?" Holly tried out thought-speaking for the first time.

"Sorry!" Helen thought back, "R and D stands for Review and Discussion groups. That's when we meet with other Souls who have had similar experiences and lessons to ours. There are usually no Guides present at an R and D group, just a group of Souls together. Souls love nothing more than to spend ages in each other's company just talking and listening and offering advice to each other. It's so useful to learn how other Souls dealt with their Life-paths."

Holly was starting to get used to the idea of communicating in thoughts now. She started wondering if she might be able to do it with some of her best friends back at school, when suddenly a thought interrupted her saying "Try it and see. It could be really fun!" She looked up and saw Helen laughing playfully at her.

"Hmmm," she thought, "it might be a little awkward if people could read *everything, all the time*! Maybe I could learn to block the private thoughts to myself?"

But she realized that Helen and probably all the other Souls could tune into her thoughts, so once again she made a mental note to be careful what she thought about in future, just in case.

"Don't worry, Hols," Helen reassured her, "up Here there are no bad thoughts, so no-one minds what you are thinking about. It's all just more learning, so let your mind go wherever it likes!"

Then Holly wondered if George was receiving all these thought messages, and quick as a flash she received a message from him too: "Yes I am, so watch what you're thinking, Jelly Brains!"

Helen acted quickly and grabbed their hands in hers before they got into a war of thought-zonking. With a quick flick of her head towards the wall, she indicated that they were about to move on. Before either even had a chance to ask where they were going ...they were already there! They had floated into another classroom, but this time there were no desks or Guides, only lots of big, comfortable cushions all over the floor with half a dozen Souls just lounging around on them, talking, or rather, think-talking, to each other.

This must be an R and D group, thought Holly, and looked at Helen, who nodded at her.

"Hi everyone!" thought Helen to the group. "Let me introduce you to my Earth sister and brother, Holly and George, who have come to spend a little time with us so they can understand Soul School a little better."

"Hello, Holly!"

"Hi, George!"

"Welcome, you two!"

"Come and join us on the cushions!"

Lots of friendly thoughts came to Holly and George from the group. They felt immediately at ease as they sat down on two very large soft cushions at the edge of the group.

One Soul propped himself up on the cushion next to her and introduced everyone out loud. As he pointed to each Soul it transformed into a shape that Holly and George could recognise as human so they could feel more at ease.

"Hi, Holly and George. My name is Zack..." said the Soul nearest to them, in thought-speak. Holly thought he looked about forty. He pointed to the other Souls one by one and introduced them, "...and this is Sarah, Zoe, Ramon, Morgan and Jayminee. We were just discussing some of the situations we used to get into when we were school kids. Would you like to join in?"

"Cool! I'd love to," thought back Holly, making lots of exaggerated movements with her face, because she found it hard to believe that the Souls would understand her if they couldn't at least *see* her miming her sentences. "That's if you don't mind?"

"'Course not!" thought Ramon, grinning at Holly's

expressions. "It's always good to meet new people."

Holly guessed that the other Souls appeared to be aged between twenty-five – Zoe – and Jayminee who looked around eighty, with a kind, wrinkled face.

"Sixty-eight, actually!" communicated Jayminee, reading Holly's thought. "I used to look really young for my age till I was about fifty-five. Then my life became rather tough for a few years so I probably aged a lot over that time, but it all came out right in the end," she added, smiling. "I can tell you about it later if you like."

"That would be really interesting," thought back Holly, pursing her lips and raising her eyebrows up and down for extra effect.

"I think it would be easier if we all spoke out loud, to begin with at least," announced Zoe, aloud, noticing Holly's facial contortions with a broad grin. "That way Holly and George will know who the voices are coming from," she added diplomatically.

"Good idea," agreed everyone.

George pulled at Helen's sleeve.

"What's up, Georgie?" she asked.

"Well, is it OK if I go outside for a while? It's just…well, my head's aching a bit from too much learning today," he said quietly.

Helen looked down at him fondly, her hand covering her mouth so he wouldn't notice her stifling a chuckle.

"Georgie, of course you can. Come on, I'll take you to meet some Souls you can play with. I'll just check with Holly to make sure she's OK with that."

She went to ask Holly if she wanted to come with them or stay in the R and D group. Holly definitely wanted to stay and said she didn't mind if Helen took George outside for a while.

"Anytime you want me to come and fetch you, just send me a message, OK?" said Helen, and with that, she took George's hand and they floated out of the classroom.

CHAPTER 11

George Takes Time Out

I n next to no time George found himself floating out over the immense marble building and crystal towers, hand in hand with Helen.

"Where are we going?" he called out.

"I'm whisking you away! " Helen replied. "You're going to meet some really cool people to play with. You'll love it!"

Before he could think what he wanted to know next, he heard Helen say, "Here we are!" and they were landing next to the enormous lake in the park.

In front of them was a long, wide strip of white sand, bordering the lake. Several rows of olive trees stood behind some small sand dunes, with scattered orange trees and wild forsythia bushes for company. George's attention was drawn to the fact that the lake had no colour to it. It seemed to be completely transparent, just like tap water in a glass. He could see right down to the bottom, and he walked slowly, intently watching the countless colourful fish meandering lazily near the surface.

"How come the water's not blue up Here?" he asked.

"Water's not blue on Earth either," laughed Helen. "Would you prefer it to be blue?"

"No, I like it like this, you can see everything, just like looking in a gigantic goldfish bowl, except with tons of fish in it!"

After walking along for a few minutes, George then noticed a volleyball game taking place over a net on the sand some distance away.

"Can we watch, Helen?" he tugged at her hand.

"Thought you might say that," smiled his sister. "You can play a bit if you like!"

"I don't really know how," said George, "and they're all much bigger than me, and they're really good..."

"Hey, you don't have to play if you don't want to, Georgie," Helen said. "We can just watch for a while first and then see how you feel, OK?

"OK," agreed George, wishing he'd been a bit bolder. The volleyballers were having a great game, and some of them didn't look so good after all, but they were still really enjoying themselves.

"Want to play yet, Super George?" she asked again after a few minutes of watching.

"Only if you play too," replied George, coyly.

"Brilliant!" she cried. "It's much more fun to play than to watch. Let's go!"

George started to take his shoes and socks off, and was

rolling the legs up of his corduroy jeans when he looked up to see where Helen was. Double take! She was standing next to him in a pale blue bikini!

"How…?" he began, but she interrupted him, laughing.

"This is Heaven remember, Georgeous! If I want to play in a bikini, I play in a bikini! What would you like to play in?"

"Um, well, it's quite hot, so have you got any shorts I could borrow…?"

"Have I got any shorts you could borrow? Hmmm, let's see know… how about those?"

"Which? Where? You haven't got any," protested George.

"That's because you're wearing them. Yeah! You look cool, Georgie boy!" Helen grinned.

George looked down and saw in place of his jeans and tee shirt he was now wearing a bright orange and brown patterned pair of beach shorts that came down to his knees.

"Too cool!" He loved them. The clothes he had been wearing just five seconds ago had somehow neatly folded themselves into a pile next to him on the grass.

"Come on, trendy beach dude, let's play ball!" Helen laughed, grabbing his hand and running on to the sandy court.

Everyone was so friendly and showed George how to hold

his hands and arms together and soon he could 'dig' the ball off his wrists and 'volley' the ball with his hands, almost in the right direction every time. He liked learning 'spiking' best. Spiking involved jumping up as high as possible at the net and smashing the ball down on the other side with the hand. He was quite a bit smaller than the others though, so Asif, one of the really good players, kept lifting him up by his waist so his head and shoulders were way above the high net. Asif had to get the timing right so George could meet the ball in mid-air and then he could spike it down as hard as he could on the other side with his fist.

Helen was having great fun too. She was wonderful at diving and rolling into the sand to stop the ball hitting the floor, and she could spike the ball seriously hard. George watched his sister with pride. He loved it that she was a good athlete. So many girls at his school couldn't even catch a tennis ball when the boys threw it to them in the playground. They spent their games lessons playing netball which was really boring because it was so easy and slow. Volleyball was a much more exciting game, he thought, and decided there and then he was going to ask his teacher to let them play at school when he went back. He hadn't even known Helen knew how to play volleyball, but she was really good at it.

"We played all the time at school," she told him, breathlessly, getting to her feet after yet another miracle dive into the sand to stop the ball touching the sand. "Best game in the Universe! You're a star for suggesting this, Georgie, I haven't played volleyball for donkeys' years. Started to forget how much fun it is!"

They had dozens of fantastic rallies with everyone throwing themselves around all over the court to keep the ball from hitting the sand. At one point, Charlie, a tall woman on the other team, accidentally spiked the ball so hard that it hit George full on the top of his head before he even had time to duck, let alone dig it. It knocked him flying backwards and he landed in a sprawling heap in the sand. His team-mates crowded round and pulled him up on to his feet again, making sure he was alright, but they had no need to worry. George was pretending he was in a movie and had been shot at by cowboys, and was staggering and falling over, making everyone laugh.

Several exhilarating minutes later and the set had finished. George's team had won by twenty-five points to twenty. The teams started to change ends, ready to play another set. Helen noticed George was puffing a bit and his cheeks were glowing.

"Come on, Champ…Time Out for you and me! Fancy an

ice cream break!" Helen suggested, brushing sand off her knees and shins.

"You bet!" said George and they said goodbye to Asif and Charlie and all their new team-mates. "That was so ace!" he carried on breathlessly, his eyes sparkling. "But where will we find an ice cream shop?"

"You big Fruit and Nut Case, there aren't any shops in Heaven," Helen reminded him. "If you want ice cream up Here, then ice cream you shall have!"

She pointed behind George's head and he looked round. There, not five feet away was indeed an ice cream stand.

"That wasn't there before!" he exclaimed.

"You didn't want any before," she replied dryly, winking at him.

"But there's no one here. Maybe it's closed."

"It's self-service, George, you can just help yourself to any flavours you want."

"For real?"

"For real."

But when George looked into the ice cream tray, all he could see was one large box of pale yellow ice cream and some cones, stacked to the side.

"They only have one flavour, Hels," he complained. "It doesn't say what it is."

"Remember where you are, Georgie? Up Here you can choose what flavour you'd like it to be," Helen reminded him, handing him a double scoop cone of pale beige ice cream. "Any flavour at all."

"So... I can have Liquorice All-Sorts flavour if I want?" asked George, dubiously.

"Take a lick," suggested Helen.

George took a long lick all around the cup of the cone, slurping up all the drips that were starting to trickle down the sides and on to his fingers.

"Coo-ooll!! It *is* Liquorice All-Sorts flavour!" he whooped, delightedly, taking several more quick licks. "But how...?" he started once again.

"Whatever flavour you want it to taste of, that's what it will taste of," explained Helen. "It's called Imagination Ice-cream."

"So if I wanted it to be Roast Lamb and Mint Sauce flavour...?"

"Would you like it to be Roast Lamb and Mint Sauce flavour?"

George opened his eyes wide, expectantly.

"So take a lick!" Helen prompted.

Sure enough, his ice cream had a distinct flavour of lamb and mint.

"'Mazing!" he grinned. He walked along next to Helen, humming happily to himself, wishing for a different flavour concoction at each lick. Mango and Butterscotch flavour, Fish and Chips flavour, Chicken Korma flavour, Christmas pudding flavour, Cup of Tea With Two Sugars flavour...he invented dozens of unlikely and far-fetched concoctions, taking a satisfying lick with each one.

"Have you proved your point yet?" asked Helen.

"Mmmm, not, mmm, yet!" replied George, slurping messily. "My imagination still has some left..." he continued, the ice cream smearing itself all over his chin and fingers.

As he came to the last few licks he suddenly started to feel distinctly queasy. His cheeks, which only minutes before had been a healthy red colour from his volleyball exertions were now a less healthy pale green.

"I think I need a glass of water," moaned George, clutching his stomach. "Quick!"

"I'm not surprised, Mister Greedy Guts!" chuckled Helen. "Lucky there's a Glass of Water Stand next to you then," she said, casually.

Right next to George was indeed...a stand with several glasses of cool water. Amazing! There really was everything you wanted, right when and where you wanted it. George made a mental note to try out some more wishes, but just…no more edible ones for a while.

He took a glass, and gulped it down in one go, plonking the empty glass back on the stand.

"Steady, Eddie!" said Helen, "Take it slow or all that ice cream you've eaten will be revisiting that cone in a minute!"

George made a smacking sound with his lips and picked up another glass. This time he sipped from it more slowly.

"That's more like it, Sticky Chops," she approved. "Now, let's just walk around the lake slowly for a little while till you feel a bit better."

He reached over and grabbed his sister's thumb, wrapping a sticky palm round it and swinging their arms backwards and forwards as they walked.

The cool lake breeze filled his lungs and he started feeling better. George wished for quite a few more water stands as they strolled round the lakeshore. He drank a glass from each as he walked thumb in palm with Helen, swinging their arms and singing silly rhymes which they made up as they walked.

A familiar squawky voice interrupted their songs.

"'One for Sorrow, Two for Joy'… that's a good rhyme to know, isn't it!"

They both turned to see two familiar magpies flying down

from some nearby trees.

"Thought it was you," called Ponke. "I said to Quok, didn't I, Quok, I said that's George and Helen by the lake there, isn't it?"

"Quok," agreed Quok.

They landed a few feet away and hopped over towards Helen and George.

"So here we are, just the two of us this time, so that'd be Joy we'd be bringing you. Two for Joy. Are you having a Joyful time, hmmm? If not, it's certainly time for some Joy. Right now. Joytime, that's what it is," persisted Ponke.

"That's very generous, Ponke, thank you. Yes we are having a fun time…"

"Fun *and* Joy, now we're both here, the two of us magpies together?" demanded Ponke.

"Fun *and* Joy," confirmed Helen.

Quok turned towards George and seemed to beckon him with a wave of his wing, before hopping down towards the lakefront. George looked towards Helen who had seen the gesture too, and she nodded her assent that he could follow. George walked down to the water's edge and stood next to Quok.

Without turning his head to face George, Quok continued looking out over the water and started to speak.

"If you look over there, you'll see something rather interesting," he said quietly.

"But... I thought... you could only say, Quok...Quok," said George, surprised and intrigued.

"What I *can* do and what I *choose* to do are two very different things, young man," continued Quok. His voice sounded very smooth and refined. "Sometimes it serves me to keep my thoughts to myself, so I do. And sometimes when I think it might be useful, I choose to share them. However, I would be ever so grateful if you kept our little secret, just that...a secret, especially from that disorderly rabble who insist on hanging around with me," he said conspiratorially. He ever so slightly inclined his head in George's direction and tapping the end of his beak with the tip of his wing. "Some secrets are best..."

"...never to be told! I know!" interrupted George, and he tapped the end of his nose with his forefinger. "Don't worry, I won't tell a Soul!"

"Oh very droll, young George, very droll," Quok said dryly. "As I was saying, right now I think you might be interested in looking towards the far side of the lake," and he pointed his large wing across the water.

George squinted into the bright lights that shimmered over the lake in the direction that Quok was pointing. In the distance he saw what he took to be a huge purple bird flying over the water. And beneath it there was what looked like a man dangling from some long strings. It seemed as if he was being dragged along, just skimming the surface and bouncing off the water.

"Helen, look!" George cried, turning to attract his sister's attention.

Helen and Ponke joined them at the waterfront and they all stopped to watch. After a few moments George could make out it wasn't a bird at all, it was a huge purple kite and it was being controlled by the man at the end of the strings, who had his feet on a small surf-board.

Excited, George shouted out towards the surfer and waved his hands.

The man spotted Helen and George and steered his kite towards them. A few seconds later, he was almost in front of them, where the shallow water met the sand. He manoeuvred his strings so the kite lost its wind and drifted down into the lake behind him, while he rode his momentum along the top of the ripples and straight onto the beach twenty yards away.

He unclipped his feet from their fastening on his board and walked over to them.

George was thrilled. He had never seen anything like it before.

"Hello," said Helen. "That was very impressive!"

"Thanks," said the young man, who looked a lot younger close up than George had first thought. About fifteen or sixteen he guessed. He had a slim, muscular body, hair down to his shoulders and under his bottom lip sprouted a little wispy goatee beard which was dyed bright blue.

"Hi, I'm Jody," he said.

"Helen," said Helen, shaking his hand. "And this is my brother George."

"Good to meet you both," said Jody, amiably.

"And…" began Ponke, a little pointedly.

"So sorry, you two," apologised Helen. "Jody, this is Ponke, and this is Quok."

"Pleased to meet you both too" said Jody, smiling.

"Likewise, young man, likewise," said Ponke, cheerfully.

"Quok," said Quok, deadpan, deliberately not catching George's eye.

"Have you ever been kite-surfing before?" Jody asked Helen.

"No, neither of us has," replied Helen. "You make it look easy, but I bet it isn't."

"Takes a bit of getting used to at first," agreed Jody. "The kite is really powerful in a good wind, you have to know what you're doing or it can get a bit hairy."

George wondered what a hairy kite would look like.

"'Hairy' can also mean 'a bit dangerous'," Helen translated, reading his thought.

"Oh, right!" giggled George, his ears turning red as they had a habit of doing when he felt he'd said something foolish.

"You want me to give you both a quick lesson?" Jody asked.

George looked pleadingly over at his sister, who had no objections at all.

"I'll pass, thanks, but I think I know someone who might take you up on that, Jody, if you really don't mind," said Helen. "I'll sit over here and watch. OK with you, Sir George?"

"Mint!" George could hardly contain his excitement. "Can I go up…you know…in the sky?" he blurted out, a little giddy with the anticipation.

"It all depends," said Jody. "Do you *believe* you can go up in the sky?" Jody threw his question back at him.

"Do I *believe* I can?" echoed George. "I don't know yet, I've never tried."

Jody waited expectantly and raised one eyebrow without saying anything.

George took the hint. "OK, yes I think I can…when you

show me!"

"Attaboy! The way I look at things is if you believe you can, you're right, and if you believe you can't, you're right too. Whatever you believe you can do, you can do!"

"Will you show me then?"

"I think we could grant that request, buddy!" replied Jody. "Follow me over here, and let's get started."

Helen watched as Jody explained all about kites, wind directions, board fastenings, harnesses - George was transfixed. Jody drew lots of diagrams with his finger in the sand and George sat next to him, soaking up every word and picture. Helen couldn't remember ever seeing him so totally engrossed in a new activity, and for George, who loved learning new things, especially new sports, that was saying a whole lot.

Helen allowed her own mind to wander as she watched George and Jody rig up the kite again. She was so proud that George and Holly were reacting so well to their visit to Soul School.

Her reflections were interrupted again by Ponke's sharp tones.

"Ladies and Gents, 'Joytime' has evidently been brought to you, courtesy of Ponke and Quok, Magnanimous Magpies to the Masses!" he announced grandly. "Come Quok, our work is done. Helen we bid you farewell."

"Farewell to you, Ponke and you, Quok," said Helen, "and thank you for bringing Jody to our attention. George is having so much fun now, thanks to you!" she was careful to add. "See you both soon I hope."

"Our pleasure to be at your service," declared Ponke, puffing out his chest. Then he hopped two-footed towards the water's edge and took off just in time to keep his feet dry.

Quok remained on the waterfront a few seconds longer. He looked at Helen, rolled his eyes almost apologetically, and without a word, took off over the water to catch up with his companion.

CHAPTER 12

R and D

Meanwhile, back in the R and D class Sarah was showing the group a lesson she'd learned from when she was young and still at school. "Give me your hands, Holly," she said.

Holly offered her hands to Sarah who placed them alongside her own, into her Red Book. As their hands touched the book Holly was excited to see all kinds of pictures and stories coming out in the light. Holly noticed Sarah was concentrating quietly and after a few seconds the pictures settled down into one particular event.

"This is where we were when you came in," explained Sarah. "Watch!"

With her hands and Sarah's in the Red Book, a story emerged in the light. Everyone in the room could see and hear the pictures that showed Sarah as a young girl in her school playground. Sarah dipped her face into the light and suddenly the whole group was transported into the story.

It seemed that Sarah was the leader of a small gang of girls and, as Holly watched and listened she understood that Sarah was behaving like a real bully to some other schoolchildren. Scene after scene emerged where Sarah was being mean, demanding money and sweets, fighting and calling people names. Holly realised that the story was unfolding over several months, even though it seemed like no time at all that they were witnessing all the key events.

Presently, Sarah transported them back out of the story, and the light disappeared back into the book.

"So, what do you think about that?" Sarah asked Holly.

"Well, you were being really nasty to those children," observed Holly, who felt a bit awkward saying what she was thinking.

"It's OK to say what's on your mind in an R and D group remember, Holly," said Zoe. "We share all our thoughts anyway!"

"Well," continued Holly, "what I was thinking was that it wasn't because you didn't like *them* very much, but more because you didn't like *yourself*."

"That's so right!" exclaimed Zack. "She was trying to make other people feel as bad as she did…"

"…so she wouldn't be the only one feeling bad…" chipped in Morgan.

"It's true," admitted Sarah. "I was always fighting with my Mum, and my Dad didn't live with us any more, so I spent years feeling really sorry for myself, especially when I met other people who seemed to have happy families. So I s'pose I used to try to make them unhappy like I was."

"What did your Guide show you when you watched this together?" asked Ramon.

"Well, he made me watch it several times, over and over," admitted Sarah. "To begin with, all I could feel were the emotions of the other children. I felt their pain when I saw myself watching them, their confusion about why someone wanted to be nasty to them, their suspicions when I told them something because they had learned not to trust anything I said. I was really uncomfortable and he asked me what I would do differently next time. After watching it through several times, I knew how much pain I had caused in so many people and I could feel that pain so strongly I knew I never wanted to feel it, or make other people feel it, ever again."

"That sounds just right," agreed Jayminee. "We have to think about how difficult it can be for other people too," she said. "For example, when your Dad left, he couldn't have been very happy either, nor your Mum. So next time, you could ask yourself what kind of behaviour they would like to see from *you*, that could help *them* feel better."

"Yes, and your school friends too," added Morgan. "They all had their own problems and challenges at home too, but they didn't all go around trying to make other people's lives miserable."

"That's a good way to look at it," said Sarah. "I never really gave any thought to how unhappy my parents were with their own situation. Or my friends, with the situation I put them in. I'm going to talk to my Guide about how I can practice being more considerate towards others in my next Life-path."

One by one, and sometimes all together, Holly's new friends contributed their suggestions and feelings towards Sarah's story. Then, in turn, they reviewed and discussed various chapters of their own recent lives. Holly entered the light with each of them, witnessing how each of them had lived through difficult situations, all while they were of school age. Stealing, telling lies, bullying, graffiti-ing, being cruel to pets – it was hard to believe that these happy, friendly Souls could have done all those things.

"Remember we were all humans too, just like you," said Zack out loud, reading her thoughts. "On Earth it's unavoidable that we'll make mistakes. The key is to be open to the learning they provide."

Holly was fascinated. But it wasn't only the negative sides of their lives that they reviewed. She was every bit as interested when they revisited the positive and uplifting moments of their life-stories too. She was completely enthralled watching and reviewing the joys and delights of their stories of immense kindness, generosity and bravery and achievement.

Time flew by with the R and D group. They involved her fully as they all shared their stories, thoughts, ideas and advice with one another. She noticed they never blamed or judged anyone which was something she wasn't used to. When she did bad things on Earth people would usually tell her off, or punish her or make her feel judged. Some of the things she had done in her life that she wasn't very proud of started to come into her mind. She quickly tried to stop the thoughts because she felt ashamed and she didn't want the group to think she was a bad person.

"Don't be hard on yourself, Holly," said Morgan cheerfully. "As you can see, we've all done things that had a bad effect on others too when we were humans. And things we weren't proud of. Helen has probably told you about the healing shower of light we all go through when we arrive back up Here…?"

Holly nodded.

"…So all the human shame and guilt and emotional suffering is washed away. What's most important, in order to benefit from our actions on Earth, is to be able to talk them through, learn from them…"

"Yes, seeing things from someone else's viewpoint makes it much easier to understand *why* they behave like they do," interrupted Zack. "That's far more interesting and satisfying than judging them, and far more useful too."

"We all mess up from time to time," added Ramon. "So it can be hypocritical to judge others or blame them when they act irresponsibly."

Holly felt very grown up sitting around and talking about things like this. She was particularly captivated with the idea of trying to understand *why* people had behaved like they had, rather than getting angry or upset with them. This way, Holly could see that people would find it much easier to do things responsibly once they understood what made them do something irresponsibly in the first place, and what effects they were having on people around them.

All of a sudden she realised she had no idea at all how long she had been in the classroom with these Souls. She had been completely absorbed by becoming involved in all their personal stories. It was so interesting learning all about how to be more considerate towards other people, but her mind started wandering towards what her brother and sister were doing now and she decided to send Helen a thought message.

Before she'd even thought what she was going to 'think'

to Helen, Helen appeared at her side.

"Wow! That was quick!" Holly blurted out, and immediately felt a little guilty about letting the group know that her mind was straying towards other things.

"Holly, don't you worry about a thing," said Morgan kindly, understanding her feelings. "You've got so much else to see up Here. I hope you've found it interesting sharing our R and D."

"Thank you so much, I mean it, really," gushed Holly. "It's been amazing meeting you all…"

"Tell us the most important thing that's struck you from this session before you go, Holly," suggested Zoe. "It's always good to wrap up an R and D session with a strong insight."

"Well…OK," began Holly, a little embarrassed at being in the spotlight.

What am I going to say? She wondered to herself, and was horrified to hear her voice start to answer anyway.

"There are so many things I've learned that are new to me, so if I had to choose the most important…" she paused to think for a few seconds, more self-consciously aware than ever that she hadn't a clue how she was going to finish her sentence.

What would my Soul say now? She found herself

wondering, and no sooner did she realise that she had asked her Soul a question, than she heard her own voice saying out loud "…it would probably be about happiness. What I mean is… that to be deep down happy, you have to treat other people the way you deep down want to be treated yourself. Happiness means different things to different people. The key is to allow yourself to take responsibility for making sure you are happy first, which allows others to relax around you. Then they can begin to create peace and calmness and happiness in their own lives too."

She looked around at the others who were smiling and nodding their heads encouragingly. She was a little dazed by what she had just said - she certainly hadn't known she was going to say all that. Despite her grand statement, her intuition told her she had been a little long-winded with her insight, and it decided she needed to wrap it all up in one short sentence.

"So I s'pose what my strongest insight is…" her voice concluded, more confidently this time, "…I will only truly find peace around me once I've made it with myself first."

Her insight was greeted with total silence from the Souls in the classroom. Holly was immediately nervous that she had said something completely wrong, but as she scanned their serene faces she detected what felt like admiration

114

passing between them, and after a few seconds, Zack turned to her and broke the silence.

"That's a truly beautiful insight, Holly, well said!" and he clapped his hands together.

"Wonderful, wise words from a wonderful, wise young woman," smiled Sarah.

"You're a very special person, Holly, it's been a pleasure meeting you," added Ramon, shaking her hand.

Holly was glowing with all the attention and compliments and she caught herself wishing George were here to hear her getting all this praise.

"Time to go, Hols. Goodbye, everyone and thanks for looking after us!" called Helen, taking her hand.

"Bye Helen, bye Holly!"

"Good Luck!"

"Take care of George too! He's so lucky to have you as his big sister!"

With the sound of friendly voices wishing her well ringing happily in her ears, Holly was still marvelling that her Soul had spoken up and revealed its wisdom at exactly the right moment. She vowed to remember to consult it again next time she felt stuck and offered it a quiet thank you, as she floated away with Helen to rejoin George.

CHAPTER 13

The Rock, The Lake And The Wind

"So where's George? Isn't he with you?"

"George is fine, Hols. Let's see now - he's been playing volleyball down on the beach by the lake, he's been eating way too much ice cream and the last I saw of him he was kite-surfing over the lake with a new friend. I think we can safely say he's having a ball," answered her sister, thinking of George's delighted face as he took off over the lake for the first time, harnessed tightly to Jody.

"There's a beach up Here too?" asked Holly, who was thinking how pleasant it would be to go for a swim in the lake right now. "And you can play volleyball? And kite-surfing?! I didn't know you could play sports in Heaven too."

"Everything up Here is simply how you want it to be, Hols," replied Helen. "You can do or play anything you like. The only rules are to have fun and be friendly."

"Mint!" exclaimed Holly. "I like those rules. Can we go to the lake after we've finished in the Library?"

"Anytime you like," Helen assured her. "You can go now if you want."

"Hmmmmm...?" Holly pondered. "Yeah, maybe I will! I

could do with a bit of fresh air – can we go back to the library later?"

"'Course we can. Come on, I'll take you."

A few moments later they were by the lakeside, on the opposite shore from where George had been learning about kite-surfing with Jody.

"It's so beautiful here!" exclaimed Holly, looking out over the crystal clear lake. A pair of goldcrests were chasing one another playfully in and out of the branches of a crab-apple tree, and she noticed a gangly stork flying low over the water, its long wings carrying it purposefully towards the oak trees on the far shore. A small breeze blew towards them, causing little waves to lap on the beach. Holly jumped back to avoid soaking her sandals. She wished she had brought some more suitable clothes so she could go paddling.

"Swim?" Helen asked, reading her thoughts.

"But I didn't bring anything to swim in," replied Holly, disappointed.

"That looks like a great outfit to me," smiled her sister. "Very you!"

"What do you…?" Holly began and then noticed her toes felt wet, and jumped back instinctively to protect her shoes.

She looked down, and, just like George earlier, was

astonished to see she was wearing completely different clothes. Not only were her feet bare, but she was now wearing a lilac and white bikini, covered by a yellow and white floral sarong which was wrapped around her and knotted above her chest. A few paces behind her on the dry part of the beach were her clothes, neatly folded and piled up.

"Wow! Coo-ooool!" she shouted.

"Ooowww oooooooo!" her voice echoed back at her a moment later off the mountains across the water.

"I LOVE this place!"

"Uuuuuhhh aaayyyy!" the lake mimicked.

Helen laughed. "Tell you what. Why don't I leave you here for a little while by yourself to capture your thoughts. I've got an R and D session coming up anyway, so I can make a start with some friends and come back and pick you up later if you like?"

"Brilliant!" said Holly, whose mind was choc full of new thoughts and ideas from all the Souls she'd been talking to.

"You'll find the lake a great companion, I'm sure. Send me a message like before, when you want me to come back."

"I will, don't worry. See you!"

Helen floated up and out of sight in the blink of an eye.

Holly surveyed her new surroundings. Leaving her pile of

clothes behind her on the beach, she paddled slowly along the water line, singing softly to herself. After a few minutes she spotted a rock a little further away from the beach surrounded by deeper water. She decided to wade out to it. If the water became too deep she resolved to take the plunge and swim out to it; there shouldn't be any scary underwater creatures up Here, she reasoned.

She waded out till the water came up to her waist. She still had some way to go before reaching the rock so she lowered her shoulders under the water and took a deep breath. Pushing her feet off the bottom she swam a slow, even breaststroke towards the rock. Thirty strokes later she touched the side of the rock and clambered up on to it, out of the water.

Its sides were smooth and there were easy hand and footholds so she made it quickly to the top of the rock. The top was fairly flat and wide and she could sit and stretch her legs out across the hard, warm stone. Behind her was a raised platform of rock, covered in soft, green moss. She propped herself up against it, tilting her head back and closing her eyes.

What an ideal sitting rock, she thought, and let her mind start to wander over all the amazing adventures she had encountered in Soul School.

"Thanks very much, I don't get many compliments these days," said a voice.

"Who said that?" asked Holly, a little startled. She sat up straight and looked around.

"I did," said the voice. "Don't get many visitors either come to that."

"Am I...am I talking to a rock??!" asked Holly, incredulously. "Or more to the point, is a rock talking to me??"

"You are and I am," replied the Rock. "You sound surprised. That happens a lot with humans."

Holly stood up and peered over the back of the platform where she had been resting her head to see if there was someone hiding on the other side of the Rock or in the water next to it. She saw no-one.

"I can never understand why people find it so hard to believe that Rocks won't be any good at conversation. After all we've been around ages."

"Well, that is true," reflected Holly. "Rocks are very old. How long have you been here?"

"Ages, like I said," replied the Rock.

"Well, I don't mean to be rude, and I know everything is so different up Here, so even though you are really old and you've been here for ages, it's just that people wouldn't expect Rocks to talk because Rocks aren't really very *alive* are they?"

"Every bit as alive as you," countered the Rock.

"No you're not! You don't have any energy, or any thoughts. How can you call that a life? Life is when you come from somewhere to...well, to wherever you live, and then you get older and then later you die and then you're... not there any more," explained Holly, faltering slightly. "Life means coming from parents or seeds or eggs. Tell me where your parents are then? Or where you were born? Or how old you are?"

"Questions, questions," sighed the Rock. "Rocks don't really take much notice of questions since it's not really necessary for us to find out anything. All I need to know is that I've been here ages. And as for being alive, I have just as much of the same energy as you do."

"How on Earth can you say you have the same energy as me?"

"Simple. I just did. And not just on Earth either," replied the Rock, not realising it was sounding a little pedantic. "Look around you. Everything in the Universe is made up of the same energy. The Lake is, the Sand is, the Wind is, the Trees are, the Animals are. I am and you are. The Souls up Here call it Soul energy, but then of course they would, wouldn't they?"

"So are you saying humans are just a more advanced form of Soul energy than other things, whether they move or not?"

"I don't really know what 'advanced' means. I'd probably just say 'more complicated.' Rocks are very simple to understand. Soul energy...Rock energy. It's all one. It doesn't much matter what it's called. And as for being born and dying and being here and then not being here you can see that can't be true either. I'm energy in a Rock shape and I'll be around ages yet. Possibly forever, however long that might be. Right here too, I imagine. I don't know how to be anything else. You're energy in a Human shape so you'll either be on Earth or you'll be up Here, but you'll still be around forever, in one form or another. Like I said, Human energy has become complicated and emotional. I've just *become*."

"What nonsense! Being emotional hasn't got anything to do with anything," stated Holly, folding her arms. "The difference is that Rocks and Water and Air and Trees and Sand and Mountains and things like you don't actually *do* anything! And if you all *did* do things, there would be no point in you getting emotional about doing them, even if you *could*!"

"You are right there, at any rate," replied the Rock. "There is no point getting emotional about anything. Getting emotional never solved a thing. And as for *not* doing things, you're right there too. I've never done anything in my life. I don't *do*. I just *am*."

"I'd go mad if I never did anything! How could I grow, how could I learn, how could I develop if I never did anything?"

"That's the beauty of being a Rock. I don't have to grow, or learn or develop. I am what I am. Which, so others have informed me, is apparently a very relaxing space in which to find oneself. I don't know any other way so I have to take their word for it.

"I mean, consider the Lake here. She has to keep moving all day long and all night. If I had anything to think with, which I don't, I'm sure I'd think that all that constant movement must be exhausting. Whatever exhausting means. Or take the Trees over there. Mostly, their trunk just gets fatter and their roots grow longer underground where no-one sees them anyway. They only get to move their branches, which I have been told is quite exciting for a Tree - except that of course I haven't a clue what excitement feels like.

"The Wind gets to travel most of all and says it meets lots of curious things. Now I don't really appreciate what curious means either but it can't be very relaxing because the Wind seems to be much more restless than most of us round here and is forever trying to make other things move. It can make the Tree branches wave and the Lake rise and fall. And it can whisk up the Sand and blow it all over the place if it wants. But it doesn't have much effect on me or my cousins the Mountains over there, and anyway it talks in a weird way, so we don't pay it much attention either really."

"I'd never really thought about things in that way before," mused Holly.

"Quite right too. People should think less. If you insist on having to learn, you should spend more time with Rocks. Life is very simple really. Knowing is noticing without thinking. Rocks don't waste good energy thinking. That's why Rocks make the best teachers."

"That might be true for Rocks, but I'm a human, we have to think about things," argued Holly.

"Well be careful. I notice that too much thinking makes you humans get emotional, so then you notice the same things but in a different way. So then what you know becomes what you *knew*, so it can't be what you know any longer. In my experience that never gets anyone anywhere at all."

"I'm sure this way of looking at things must work for

Rocks, but I have to say I find it very confusing," said Holly, diplomatically. She scratched her head, which was starting to spin with the Rock's peculiar logic. "And, if you don't mind me saying so, you haven't had any experience of doing anything at all, and you've never been anywhere at all, other than being right there in the Lake," reasoned Holly.

"Precisely my point. I just am. Right here in the Lake as you have correctly noticed. That is all there is to know. Once one knows one is where one belongs, one is best staying there to appreciate it," replied the Rock. "If one starts *thinking* about where one is, one finds it changes each time and one will never know whether one belongs there or not."

"Er...I see..." began Holly, not wishing to appear impolite but feeling the need to trade these mental exercises for some physical ones. "Thank you for explaining things to me. It's been very nice talking with you. I think I will go for a swim now."

"As you wish," replied the Rock. "You are welcome to visit any time you want. Goodbye."

"Thank you, you've been very...educational, goodbye, and...good luck" said Holly, immediately wondering why she was wishing luck to a Rock that never moved, but thinking she ought to say something polite nonetheless. She clambered back down the Rock's edge and lowered herself once more into the warm, clear water and pushed off with her feet.

After a few dozen strokes she stopped to tread water, peering down into the waters at the shoals of flamingo guppys and red-tailed rainbowfish swimming care-free amongst the hairgrass on the sandy bed.

Mmmmmm, sooo-ooo-ooo relaxing! she thought, gently waving her arms and legs under the water slowly to stay afloat.

"I'm so glad you're back," said another voice. "I knew you wouldn't want to stay too much longer with the Rock."

Holly looked behind her, although somehow she wasn't startled this time.

"Don't tell me, you're the Lake talking to me, aren't you?" she guessed. "Does everything speak up Here?"

"Yes to the first and yes to the second," replied the Lake. "Everything speaks on Earth too actually, if you are just prepared to listen. I can see you are enjoying your swim."

"Oh, it's just what I needed. There's so much going on up Here and it's quite hard to take it all in and make sense of it. And…" she lowered her voice slightly, "I hope I didn't upset the Rock by leaving so soon, it's just, well, I came out here to relax and try and make sense of all my thoughts, and after a few minutes with him, they were in danger of being more jumbled up than before."

"It's normal. Rocks are for boys."

"I beg your pardon?"

"Rocks are for boys. Water's more for girls."

"Whatever do you mean?" asked Holly.

"Well like you said to the Rock, humans have to think about things so they can learn and grow. He doesn't know about thinking. He doesn't move. He…"

"He just *is*. Yes I know that, he told me. Several times."

"And you notice we both naturally refer to the Rock as 'him.'"

"So we did. And he referred to you as 'she.'"

"And so he should. He's known me for a very long time. Boys appreciate what Rocks are, you see. Boys pick them up and throw them, they climb them, they jump off them, they build things and make statues with them."

"Girls can do those things too."

"Yes they can, although when you have all finished, the boys understand the Rock's energy in a different way to girls. Rock energy is strong, hard, still, and silent. Deep inside, boys identify with that more."

"Do they? I've never really thought about that."

"In the same way that girls identify with Water."

"What way is that?"

"A girl's energy is far more in tune with mine – never truly at rest, never truly quiet. I can't be captured or resisted or transformed into anything else. I will comfort, sustain, nourish and calm. But only as long as I'm *not* still. If I'm still for too long I stagnate. Girls appreciate those energies more instinctively than boys.

"Boys need to swim against my currents, to hold their breath underwater as long as they can, to dive down and try to touch my beds, to ride my waves and try to master me. Girls can do those things too, although the excitement wears off quicker for them. They prefer to let me wash over them - they find it soothing not to battle against me. They recognise naturally how to just accept me as I am."

"I suppose you might have a point. After all, you *are* Water so you should know what you are talking about. And I am feeling very comfortable and calm now you come to mention it."

"Well make the most of it, because if the Wind changes its mood, I might have to be a little choppy for a while."

"Doesn't that bother you, having to change according to what mood the Wind chooses?" asked Holly. She was so engrossed that she didn't even realise that it was strange to be talking about the Wind *having* moods at all.

"Oh far from it! It's exciting never knowing what's going

to happen from one minute to the next. So long as I'm moving I'm happy. If it's not the Wind, it's the Fish or the Plants or the Animals that will keep me moving. Rocks have boys' energy, water has girls'. The Wind has a child's energy. It never stays in one mood for very long and it's always trying to make things do what it wants. It doesn't get on very well with Rocks because it can't get any reaction from them – whatever mood the Wind is in, the Rock ignores it. And the Wind hates to be ignored by anything. The Wind can see every part of the world there is to see, anytime it wants…"

The Lake paused to let this sink in, and then added, "…except two. Can you guess?"

Holly considered this for a moment.

"I can't think of any place the Wind couldn't find a way to reach, if it really wanted to,"

"Underwater and underground!" said the Lake almost sounding smug. "Finds it very frustrating too."

"I imagine it would. Is that why it tries to whip up waves, so it can see underneath?"

"Right. Although no matter how much water it throws around, it can't quite grasp the fact that more water will just take its place, so it's never going to win that battle. And it's found its way into some deep Caves too. But it can't get to see what the Tree roots see. Sometimes it pulls a Tree right out of the ground to get a closer look although it doesn't get to see much even then!"

Holly couldn't help thinking of the similarities with her little brother's behaviour sometimes when he didn't get what he wanted. And her own too, if she was really honest.

"There isn't much Wind right now. What mood is it in right now?"

"Well to be fair, up Here the Wind doesn't get nearly as excitable as down on Earth. Everything is much calmer up Here, and the Wind sort of accepts that. And remember that all Water up Here is crystal clear anyway so the Wind can get a pretty good look at what's underneath the surface anyway if it wants. It gets a bit peeved that the Rock can see above and below the Water without even trying though.

"But don't be fooled by its childish moods – that's just its nature. The Wind is the most well-travelled of all energy-beings and is a creature of action rather than words. However, when it does talk it is usually very enlightening. It speaks very well and sees itself as somewhat of a poet so I'm sure it will introduce itself before long."

Holly was silent for a while, floating almost effortlessly on her back in the Lake. She had never considered things from a Rock's point of view before, nor a Lake's, nor the

Wind's come to that. Even though they are so different, they all seem to just accept themselves as they are and tolerate each other, she thought.

Just as she allowed her body to drift with the Lake's warm currents, so her mind drifted too. She found herself thinking about how a Tree might see its role or its purpose in the world. She resolved to ask her Poppy Tree sometime. Or what about Flowers or Bees or... a Train or a House? She wondered what the world might look like through their eyes and their thoughts.

She didn't mind in the least that the Wind hadn't joined in on their conversation. All she wanted to do was to lie back and let the Lake transport her - she felt safe and was sure it wouldn't let her come to any harm.

The Lake understood her need and supported her willingly. Holly closed her eyes and almost fell asleep as she floated, her thoughts swimming around in her head as curiously as the tiny black angel fishes that had approached to inspect her toes. When she opened her eyes some minutes later she found that the Lake had carried her to within a few metres of the spot on the Beach where her clothes were still neatly folded and piled up.

Holly stood up in the warm Water, her bare toes curling over some scattered Pebbles on the Lake bed.

"S'cuse me? Hello up there! S'cuse me?" Several high-pitched, squeaky voices gurgled up to Holly's ears.

"Now who was that, this time?" asked Holly, but more amused than surprised this time.

"Only us," squeaked the voices. "We're the Pebbles. Could you pick us up and throw us somewhere else, we'd love a complete change of scenery if you don't mind, rather than just rolling around in more or less the same place with the Currents?"

"Well, yes I'm sure I could," Holly said, bending down. "How many of you would like to go? There are so many of you."

"All of us," squeaked the Pebbles. "It won't take long, we promise. We'd love to know what flying feels like so you can throw us as high and as far as you like."

"OK, here goes," said Holly and she scooped up several handfuls of Pebbles and flung them as high and as far as she could, away from the shore into the deeper Water.

"Wheeeeeeeeeeee! Woooohoooooo! Yipppeeeeeee!" screeched the Pebbles as they flew through the air and landed with little plops in the Lake several metres away. "This is soo-oooooo fuuuuu-uuuunnnnn!! Thanks a lot!" they gurgled at her from their new resting places on the Lake bed.

"My pleasure," called Holly making sure she didn't miss any, and watching as they all landed in a new spot in the Lake.

"Oooohhh! That tickles," now it was the Lake's turn to call out as the Pebbles hit her surface and sank to the bottom. "Lovely, more ripples, just what I needed."

Holly watched the ripples circling outwards, growing larger and thinner. They had all but disappeared by the time they had reached where she was standing. It made her smile wondering whether a Lake might feel similarly to how George reacted when she tickled him.

She turned to look out over the horizon and took in the far shore, the Rocks, the Trees and the friendly Lake. She was transfixed for a few minutes by the sight of shoals of gold-spotted swordtail fish swimming close to her feet and occasionally bumping against her legs. Not thirty metres away dozens of rare butterfly fishes flew in and out of the water, like living, bouncing rainbows. As if applauding the spectacle, two enormous purple and white striped butterflies flutter-danced appreciatively above the water, while taking good care to remain just out of range.

Further along the beach a guard of magnificent oak trees stood solemnly. Above their heavy branches, a raucous gang of magpies bickered in their customary, endearing way, silhouetted against the sky, across which brilliant messages of devotion flashed in every direction.

The Wind chose this moment to make itself known with a barely perceptible caress across Holly's face. In that caress was wrapped a moment of timeless revelation – the moment when Holly became aware that the world began to make sense.

Everything was in its rightful place, everything was at peace. Everything was at ease just being itself and enjoying everything else being itself too. Everything understood its own purpose, and knew its own beauty.

The Wind whispered into her ears.

"Look around – can you see that beauty and happiness are everywhere? Now can you understand the true nature of the Universe? I've been around it myriad times and this much I know. Beauty and happiness are the building blocks of Soul-energy which in turn is the building block of every thing, every thought. Thus every thing, animate and seemingly inanimate is, in its essence, everything else. Lavish love on one thing, every other is love-laden. Wound and you wound yourself likewise. In truth, the Universe is flawless... whenever you wish it to be so."

Holly stood stock still in the warm water for a few minutes letting her mind take in this new insight. A few days ago she could never have contemplated an idea as enormous as that. She found it hard to imagine herself standing in the playground at school discussing 'The Soul of the Universe' with her friends, as if it were no more unusual than discussing clothes, or hairstyles or boys. Up Here, right now, there seemed nothing more normal or more obvious.

After a while, inevitably her thoughts shifted and she found herself wondering where George might be now. She scanned the Lake but couldn't see him kite-surfing anywhere. She knew that, whatever he was doing, he'd be having fun and wished that Helen would come back now.

"No sooner thought than done!" said her sister, appearing behind her simultaneously. "Had a good time?"

Holly threw her arms around Helen in a big hug. "I don't know where to start first," replied Holly, "I'm sort of seeing the world in a different way though, that's for sure."

"I knew the Lake would look after you," said Helen, with a twinkle in her eye.

"Oh she did, and I had an interesting chat with the Rock too, although I'll have to think a bit harder about his point of view. And the Wind sort of brought all the pieces together – I've got so much to think about," gabbled Holly.

"All in good time," said Helen, understandingly. "And there was I thinking you were just going to relax for a while!"

"Well, I thought I was too, but even though I've been finding out all sorts of new things to think about, everything seems so much clearer somehow, and I am feeling probably more relaxed than ever."

"Clarity lodges serenity as willingly as chaos lodges angst," offered the Wind.

"Beautifully put, Wind old friend, you of all things being best placed to understand the contrasts, I'm sure!" said the Lake, coming as close to irony as a Lake is able. "My inkling is the Rock would agree wholeheartedly too," it added, somewhat labouring its point.

"No thing is that shouldn't be, nor happens without reason," countered the Wind. "Coincidence is impossible since every action has a design and every design, a consequence. Remember I too played my part in summoning our visitors."

Helen intervened quickly, in case the Wind should change his mood and spoil the moment with a petulant squall.

"Yes, thank you, Wind, for rearranging the honeysuckle petals earlier, and thank you both for enlightening my sister with your wisdom. Now, however, you must excuse us, as we should be getting back to the Library. Ready, Hols?"

"Ready," agreed Holly. "Goodbye to all of you, I'm really

grateful for everything you've taught me."

"Gratitude is growth with grace," the poetic Wind persisted, "and the key to every conundrum. Allow it to serve you well and often."

The Lake bowed out of the conversation, courteously allowing the Wind's last wise words to linger, and burbled contentedly to herself.

CHAPTER 14

Understanding Challenges with Old Harry

I t no longer surprised Holly that just by thinking about being back in the Library Halls, they quickly found themselves in another vast corridor surrounded by books of all different shapes and sizes. She was dressed in her own clothes again too.

"What colour do these books look to you?" Helen asked.

"Green," said Holly. "Are these more Life Lessons?" she wanted to know although what she really wanted was to look inside as many books as she could to hear more Soul stories.

"No, Hols, these are slightly different. The Green Books are called Life *Choices*," said Helen. "We study them to see what sort of Life-path we might like to choose to live next time. We can plan what we want to learn, who we want to meet, the family we want to be born into, the special talents and gifts we want to have. We can plan all the happy, fun things we want to experience in our lives as well as how we want to react to the more unhappy and unfortunate circumstances.

"It's up to me and my Guide to decide when I feel ready to start working on my next Life Choices. At the moment I'm still enjoying going to R and D sessions with other Soul groups, so my Guide has given me permission to show you the Library, but he says it's not helpful to look inside any Life Choice books until I feel I don't need the R and D groups any more.

"And that goes for you too, Miss Itchy Fingers...!" she laughed, grabbing Holly's hand which was inching towards a small, fat book on the shelf next to her.

"So the Red Books are about lessons from lives already lived and the Green Books are about ideas for lives yet to be lived," summarised Holly, excitedly, almost certain she was beginning to understand what Soul School was really all about. If there really were secrets that the magpies held, she was sure she must be on the right track to finding them.

"That's exactly what they are," replied Helen a little too loudly, so happy her sister had understood that she completely forgot to lower her voice too. She noticed a number of studying Souls looking right in her direction and waved her hand towards them to apologise for interrupting them, and they turned back to their studies.

"Now then, now then, now then!" barked a gruff man's voice from behind Holly, making her jump. "What be all this commotion about then?"

Holly spun round on her heel and found herself face to face with an elderly, white-haired man, not a lot taller than she was, a little portly, with a smiley, kind, wrinkled face and a thick white moustache with the ends rolled into little circles.

"Sorry, Harry, I was just so proud of Holly for understanding things so quickly I forgot where we were for a moment," laughed Helen. "Holly, this is Old Harry, my handsomest and most intelligent Guide. Harry, meet my scrumptious sister, Holly."

"Right special pleased to be meetin' you, young lady," said Old Harry, offering his hand.

"Hello," said Holly politely, taking hold of two of his fat fingers and shaking them slowly.

"An' you can be stoppin' with all that flatt'ry nonsense too, young Helen. Don't think I'll be lettin' you get your pretty little nose into them Life Choices no quicker on account of a few compliments neither!" he told her firmly, turning slyly towards Holly and winking at her, just as Helen started to object.

"I had no intention…" Helen began to declare her innocence, then caught herself. "You little teaser, Harold! I should have seen that coming." She laughed again and pinched both his cheeks lightly with her thumbs and forefingers.

Holly immediately warmed to Old Harry, it was fun to see

Helen get a taste of her own medicine.

"How do you get to become a Guide, Harry?" she asked him politely. "Is it when you have learned all the Life Lessons from all the Life Choices?"

"Well now, that be an interesting question, me duck," Old Harry started to reply. "See here…"

Helen interrupted. "Harry, Holly, I'm just going to go and check up on George by the lake. I can see that you two are going to get on famously, so I'll leave you to all Holly's questions for a little while, Harry, OK?" She wagged her finger towards his face as she warned him playfully. "And you'd better be on your toes young Harold, because believe you me, she comes out with some Ter-Rif-Ic questions, you'll see!"

And with an impish smile on her angelic face, Helen floated off to find George.

Holly was smiling at Helen for calling this elderly man 'young Harold'. She thought he looked at least sixty years old, but she could sense that they were very close.

"A right stick of dynamite that one," he complained as Helen disappeared from view. "Cheeky little Cherub, always has been!"

"How long have you known each other," asked Holly, intrigued.

"Oh, that'll be yonks and yonks, must be now…several lifetimes at least," replied Old Harry. "Don't know what I'd do with meself if I didn't have to be keepin' the mischief away from that one! But one thing I knows good and right - she loved bein' a big sister to you and Master George this time around!"

"I loved her being my sister too," said Holly, ruefully. But her mind was reeling. *Several lifetimes*! He was the second Soul to say the same thing. It couldn't really be true… could it? What if it…was? She just had to ask another question out loud, just to clarify what Old Harry had said.

"So…have I known her before too, you know, in a previous lifetime?" she blurted out, feeling a bit strange even hearing herself say the words.

"'Course you has, me duck, a lot more times'n once, if I's not mistaken. You sticks by them as you learns from best. Every Soul do. But that's all I's at liberty to tell you about your lives with her, so no more questions on that subject, does you hear me?"

"I hears you, er…hear you, Harry," said Holly, unable to resist teasing Old Harry like her sister had done.

"Now then, Missy" said Old Harry slowly, giving her what he intended to be a long, stern stare for her cheeky imitation. "What was it you was asking me again?"

"About becoming a Guide." Holly flashed him her sweetest smile. "Do you have to have learnt *all* the Life Lessons from *all* the Life Choices?"

"No you surely doesn't!" replied Old Harry. "Well, that is, *I* certainly hasn't. In actual fact a Soul can become a Guide more or less any time it chooses. You chooses to become a Personal Guide what helps or protects people when they gets really stuck Downstairs. Or you chooses to become a Soul Guide like me, and stays Upstairs, working with them as arrives fresh up Here. There be a lot of challenges in front of those, an' that's the truth. So..."

"Umm, Harry, so what *exactly* do you mean by `*challenges*'?" Holly interrupted. The word came up often in the R and D group and she was determined to put every last bit of the Soul School jigsaw in its place if she could.

"I's beginning to see that that sister of yours weren't too far wrong about you and your questions, young Miss. But you's right bein' curious and speakin' up, me duck, no-one ever got wise in silence!"

He rolled the ends of his moustache between his thumbs and forefingers, pensively. "Let me see now...challenges. Yep, a challenge means somethin' that's tricky for us to try to do," explained Old Harry carefully, "an' it gives us an opportunity to see how we copes. Then we learns lessons

144

from how we's coped. Yep, that's about the shape of it."

"So… a challenge for me and George, and Mum and Dad, is… trying to cope with Helen not being with us at home any more?" Holly asked, feeling sad again.

"That be a right fine example of what a challenge be," nodded Old Harry, putting one hand on her shoulder and squeezing it softly to comfort her. "And how is you all copin' with that?" he asked gently.

"But sometimes we're not coping very well at all – Mum's often crying, I'm lonely without her and Dad's just very quiet a lot of the time," sniffed Holly.

"Sometimes it do take time to be makin' sense of challenges," said Old Harry slowly. "When you an' your Mum an' Dad was last up Here in the Green Hall with your own Guides, it must have been important for you all to be choosin' Life-paths together, involvin' the challenges of copin' with grief, unexpected like."

On hearing that comment, Holly couldn't hold the myriad of thoughts that had been swirling around inside her head any longer. They spilled out of her mouth. Loudly.

"That's too freaky!! First Helen and now you. You're both saying I've had lots of previous lives and been up Here before!!" she almost shrieked the words. "And Mum and Dad too!! But that's impossible! I can't remember a thing about it, and they've never once said anything about it either. And I would never have chosen a life that involved losing my big sister so young!" she finished sulkily, folding her arms across her chest.

Several Souls and their Guides looked up when they heard Holly's outburst and Holly felt more than a bit sheepish. I'll definitely get told off this time, she thought. But when she glanced over in their direction and saw their kind, supportive faces it seemed they understood that she had been invited to visit Soul School to help her cope with losing her big sister. She felt Old Harry's small, chubby hand squeeze her shoulder gently once more, and she tried to compose herself.

Old Harry was smiling kindly too. "Hardly no-one remembers about bein' in Soul School once they gets back down to Earth," he explained patiently. "Nor the lessons an' challenges they chose with their Guides. Some young 'uns does remember for up to a few years but when they talks about it most other folks doesn't take 'em seriously, so they usually stops. An' after a time, them young 'uns has so many other things to think about every day that *they* starts to forget an' all."

Holly had finally run out of questions for the first time since she had arrived with the magpies. She stayed silent for ages, while she thought really hard, trying to make sense of what she was hearing.

After what seemed like forever, she looked up. "Will I forget too…you know, when I get back to Earth this time?"

Old Harry looked right into her greeny-blue eyes holding her gaze in silence for a few moments before saying simply, "Yep, me duck, you surely will."

Again, Holly took some time to let this sink in.

"So let me get this straight. You're saying that in Soul School we choose all the lessons and challenges we want to experience on Earth…" she began.

"That we does," confirmed Old Harry.

"…and then we programme ourselves to *forget* what they were once we *arrive* on Earth!" finished Holly, trying to find some logic in this chain of events.

"That we does too," confirmed Old Harry, a wry smile across his face.

"So wouldn't our lives be easier and more, well…friendly…" she continued, thinking of how friendly everyone had been in the R and D session, "…if we programmed ourselves to *remember* what we were here for when we arrived? On Earth I mean."

"Got to admit, sounds logic enough put like that," Old Harry shrugged. "Powerful feasible that'd be."

"So…?" demanded Holly, folding her arms across her

chest.

"Triffic question, Holly, one of your best so far, an' no mistake! It ain't an easy answer neither, but I'll share you what I thinks."

"What you *think,* Harry?! I thought Soul Guides were supposed to *know* everything," Holly teased boldly, her arms still folded and tapping her foot loudly too, to make her point.

"I see as you've learnt your ribbing from that sister of yours, an' that's the truth," Old Harry replied evenly. "Now does you want me to share you or not?"

"Yes, go on…share me," said Holly, not really sure if she'd used his strange phrase correctly, and hoping that it meant he was going to give her the answer to her question.

As it turned out she was right on both counts.

"The way I sees it is that we needs to work out our Downstairs things Downstairs…"

"Does 'Downstairs' mean 'on Earth'?" interrupted Holly.

"It do, me duck. Upstairs is for Upstairs and Downstairs is for Downstairs."

"I don't have a clue what you mean, Harry. You're talking gibberish."

Old Harry sighed and muttered to himself, "Surely got me work cut out with just one of these cheeky Cherubs, darned if I can be caterin' for two!"

"What did you say, Harry, I didn't catch it?" asked Holly, demurely.

"Right. Here goes, Missy," Old Harry continued, a little more haughtily than before. "An' I'll be ignoring your little jibes so you needn't go wastin' your puff."

Holly pulled a face.

"Listen tight now. Upstairs we Souls knows everythin' about everythin'. We knows who we is and what we's all about. There ain't no more learnin' necessary for a Soul Upstairs."

"So why do we need to come Downstairs, I mean to Earth, at all then, if we know everything about everything already?"

"'Cos knowin' is diff'rent from doing, young Holly. Mighty diff'rent."

Holly frowned

"Don't make no sense yet, eh?" asked Old Harry.

She shook her head.

"Let me ask you a question then," said Old Harry patiently. "Would you say you sees yourself as a kind person?"

"Well, I try to be…most of the time…" replied Holly.

"So would you say you can be *un*kind, some of the time?"

"Um… I suppose…some of the time…" began Holly, blushing a little, as lots of little thoughts of occasions she had been unkind, unfair, and unreasonable entered her mind.

"'Xactly, me duck, 'xactly! So the only way you knows that you's *being* kind, is if you knows what unkindness *feels* like too! You needs to *experience* who you *ain't* so's you can *know* who you *is.*"

"Now I…" Holly faltered. She was starting to wish she had never asked the question in the first place.

"Upstairs there's only knowin' an' bein'. There ain't no feelin' nor no doin'. Just knowin an' bein'.."

"So…we have to come Downstairs to *experience* what being and knowing *feels* like?" asked Holly, tentatively.

"'Xactly! You's got it, 'xactly! Now then, you asked me a triffic question a while back, but it's slipped my mind again…"

"Harry!" Holly reproached him impatiently. "You were saying that in Soul School we choose all the lessons and challenges we want to experience on Earth and then we programme ourselves to *forget* what they were once we arrive on Earth. So my question was why wouldn't we programme ourselves to *remember* what they were once we arrive on Earth? Surely that's a lot more logical."

"Aha, yes indeed. That was it, that was it. Well, if we

was to know Downstairs, on Earth as you calls it, what we'd planned Upstairs, up Here like, there'd be no challenges worth workin' towards. There has to be *surprise* in a challenge, otherwise we knows what's comin' at us. So Downstairs, it's important that we has to work it out cold, immediately it comes along an' hits us. An' that's how we gets to discover how we's goin' to respond to it, an' how well we's goin' to be copin' with it. An' *that's* where the learnin' be."

Holly had to admit, that Old Harry's answer made a lot of sense, even though she couldn't help thinking her English teacher would have had a nervous breakdown listening to his grammar. She cast her mind back to when Helen had asked her whether she would live her life differently if she knew for certain it was the only one she was going to get.

But Old Harry hadn't quite finished yet.

"What you has to remember, young lady, is that when things gets difficult Downstairs and you thinks you isn't sure exactly what to do…"

"You mean when I meet *challenges*?" interrupted Holly once again.

"Indeed, me duck, indeed" Old Harry ploughed on. "Anytime you meets a challenge Downstairs, and you's not 'xactly sure what to do or how to start, what you *can* remember is two things:

"One, that you gets to choose your attitude towards what you's doin'. If you approaches your challenges Downstairs with a powerful strong attitude, with maybe a bit of mischief thrown in time to time like your sister always done, life Downstairs be a right delight – as fun and joyful as life Upstairs, an' that's the truth."

It had always been fun being round Helen, Holly mused to herself.

"What was the second thing then?" she asked.

"What's that, Flower? What second thing is that?" asked Old Harry, absent-mindedly.

Holly took a deep breath to keep herself calm. "You said there were two things to remember when someone is not sure what to do, and you only told me one…" she reminded him, pointedly.

"Oh aye, that be right, now then," began Old Harry, who could definitely be a little forgetful sometimes. "What did I say the first thing was again?"

"Oh, Harry!" said Holly, exasperated. "You said we can choose our attitude towards how we approach our challenges…"

"Yep, that I did…and, errrr…oh yes, Two is, that you always has a *choice* of how hard you's goin' to try to approach 'em. That be it."

Old Harry fell silent, a look of satisfaction on his face. It seemed he had finally completed his explanation.

But Holly wasn't satisfied yet, by a long chalk. "So...what happens if I try really hard and have a positive attitude?" she continued.

Old Harry sighed, then laughed. "Then you learns a boatload about copin' with tricky challenges, doesn't you! An' your life will move along right nicely. An' next time you meets a similar challenge you'll have an 'ead start, won't you!"

"And so what happens if I'm negative?" persisted Holly, who always needed to see both sides.

"Then that teaches you somethin' important about yourself too, doesn't it, my dear? Next time you meets a challenge, you has to waste time thinkin' about what you's taught yourself from *not* trying last time!"

She saw that Old Harry had a twinkle in his eye as he was talking and she wasn't sure if he considered it was such a serious subject as she did. But there seemed to be so many things she still needed to know, and he'd all but given her permission to ask as many questions as she needed.

This one just blurted itself out before she could stop it. "But how will I even *recognise* a challenge when I meet one, anyway?!"

Old Harry had been enjoying Holly's earnest attempts to get to the bottom of things - she definitely was keeping him on his toes. This last question however just made him laugh out loud.

Helen and George floated back into view just as Old Harry burst out laughing.

Old Harry had one of those deep, bubbly, brassy laughs that sounded like a tuba being played underwater. All the Guides and Souls within earshot turned to see what was happening. Even Helen looked a little sheepish and Old Harry covered his mouth with one hand and then the other on top to try and keep the noise in. Holly could see his eyes and they seemed to be laughing all by themselves as well. It was an infectious laugh and Helen, George and even Holly herself just had to laugh along too.

Helen hugged her little sister once again. "I just knew you two would get on like bears in a honeypot!" she said, still chuckling happily.

"Holly, my dear," said Old Harry, between tuba bubbles. "This be my advice. Anytime you thinks somethin's tricky, just ask yourself how hard you's goin' to try to achieve it or cope with it. Then it doesn't matter if it be a challenge or it ain't – you still knows exactly what you's goin' to do, an' that's the truth!"

Helen tugged on George's sleeve, pulling him out from behind her. He was still giggling at this funny old man with the white moustache and the big laugh.

"George, this is my Guide I was telling you about, he's called Harry," said Helen. "Harry, meet my brother George."

Old Harry offered his hand and George took it and shook it hard.

"What do you know, young Master?" asked Old Harry, pleasantly.

"Um…I know…you've got a mad laugh and you talk weirdy," George said to Old Harry matter-of-factly.

"George!" warned Holly, reprovingly.

"Delighted to meet you too, young Master," replied Old Harry, his tuba-laugh bubbling up again. "I has a feelin' we's all goin' to get along powerful peachy!"

CHAPTER 15
All Together Again

Although they could float to anywhere they wished in the blink of an eye up Here, sometimes there was more fun to be had on foot. All four of them had decided to walk the short distance to the magical meadow in which the two young visitors had landed.

George was on one of his famous 'energy highs' as Mum called them. There was no stopping him. Holly and Harry had little choice but to hear every last excited detail of his time by the lake: "...beach volleyball... imagination ice-cream... swimming... new friends... Jody... kite-surfing... blue goatee... singing songs round a campfire... toasting marshmallows and drinking cocoa... zonking..."

"Wait!" shrieked Holly, when he reached this part. "You taught them zonking??!!"

"Yeah! It was too cool! At first they weren't very good at it because they told me no-one's used to insulting people in Heaven," George told his amused audience. "But when I explained that zonking isn't being rude, it's just sort of being cheeky with words, they all thought it was the funniest thing ever. They got the hang really quickly and when I left everyone was zonking everyone else!"

"Sounds like young Master George is right powerful at makin' friends, an' that's the truth," Old Harry chortled, sincerely.

"Mum's always telling him not to talk to strangers," Holly tittle-tattled. "He keeps getting in trouble for it."

"Up Here strangers is just kinfolk we hasn't yet come to meet," Old Harry informed no-one in particular.

"What's a 'kinfolk'?" asked George.

"Kinfolk means family," Helen explained.

"Oh," said George, intrigued. "So up Here, strangers are family we haven't met yet," he translated, more for his own benefit than for anyone else. "Too cool! If that was the same on Earth I could talk to *everyone* and not get into trouble!"

"Don't even think about it!" sighed Holly.

Actually, Holly was really happy to see George back again although she was more than a little envious of the fun he'd had while she'd been doing R and D in Soul School. Despite telling tales on him (which just seemed to happen all by itself) Holly had to admit she'd missed him, even though he drove her nuts like no-one else at times. But he also made her laugh like no-one else too, he was very bright for his age, and he really was very good-natured. Plus she was his big sister after all, so if she didn't look out for him, who would?

She knew he couldn't be expected to have the patience to understand everything she'd seen in the R and D sessions and the green Hall, nor all the things she'd discussed with Old Harry. She felt genuine fondness seeing him so relaxed and happy, and she was trying her best to listen as attentively as she could to his breathless stories.

The trouble was, her mind wanted to concentrate on something entirely different. Despite herself, she soon tired of being a good listening sister, and she took hold of Helen's hand and slowed her walking pace down just a fraction. Still chattering away nineteen to the dozen, George got a little way ahead with Old Harry, so now she had Helen all to herself.

"OK, Miss Terious, spill the beans!" Helen sensed something was on her sister's mind.

Holly was getting used to her sister reading her thoughts so she looked up at Helen, not really sure why she was feeling nervous. But she was.

"Umm, it's just, well… you know that nice, smiling young woman I saw in our living room, and the magpies, and this whole visit to Soul School…all the things I've learned up Here…"

"Go on," said Helen.

"Well, Old Harry says I'm going to forget everything

159

when I go back home, I mean Earth home, not Home up Here, and…" At the same moment she said the word 'home' her eyes welled up with tears all of a sudden. She remembered again that nobody knew where she was, and they would definitely be really worried about where she and George had disappeared to. And the other reason was that she didn't want to leave Helen, now she'd found her again.

"Don't worry about any of it, Hols," soothed Helen comfortingly, once again reading Holly's anxious thoughts. "First of all, it might seem like you've been up Here ages and ages, but on Earth it's been no time at all. Time is completely different up Here. Mum and Dad won't have missed either of you yet, *not one bit*! And I'll always be watching over you *I promise*. Wherever you are, whenever you need me, I'll be there."

Holly relaxed a little. "You're sure, *sure*?" she asked, catching a sniffle with the back of her sleeve.

"Sure, sure, *sure*!" promised Helen. "And secondly, no, you won't exactly forget *everything* you've learned up Here," she continued. "The wisdom stays with you down there for when you have need of it. Harry meant you'll just forget *how you learnt it*, that's all. Remember, your own Guide travels with you wherever you are. If you have questions, on Earth especially, you just need to find a quiet place somewhere and ask her what you need to know. Make sure you take the time to listen to what she tells you. Whatever happens she'll always get an answer back to you."

"How do you know who my Guide is?" Holly asked, "*I've* never seen her."

"She's around pretty much all the time, Hols, she's called Sophie. She's talked to you many times too. And actually you *have* seen her, just once, and very recently."

"I have??" asked Holly, "when…?"

"If you think back a few sentences, you'll remember…" replied Helen, smiling mysteriously.

"Helen! Stop *teasing* and just *tell* me!" said Holly crossly, stamping her foot and folding her arms across her chest.

Helen looked fondly at her sister, saying nothing but smiling broadly.

Helen's silence gave Holly time to reflect. Suddenly it came to her – "the smiley woman…in the living room…the honeysuckle blossom…that was…Sophie??!!"

"That was Sophie," confirmed Helen, her eyes twinkling at Holly. "You may never actually *see* her again, but you only have to ask her questions and you'll hear her answers in your mind," Helen said. "And of course, find a quiet place to listen too."

Up ahead, George had just about talked himself out. Old

Harry knew so much about beach volleyball and kite-surfing now from George he almost considered taking a wander over to the lake himself later on and joining in.

Old Harry had noticed a change in the air, and as they walked along he licked his forefinger and held it out in front of him.

"Just as I thought," he murmured, under his breath. He took advantage of a rare gap in George's endless burbling.

"Anyone like to be comin' to a party?" he asked out loud, turning back towards the others.

"'Mazing! What kind of party?" George asked back, instantly forgetting what he'd been bending Old Harry's ears about for the last twenty minutes, now there was fresh excitement to be had.

"Touch my finger, young Master George," he said, holding it in front of George's face.

George reached out, wondering what kind of game Old Harry was playing and grabbed hold of the stubby, leathery finger.

Zzzzaaappp!! Little sparks flew up and George jumped backwards, shaking his hand which was tingling madly.

"Whoh! What was that??!" he exclaimed, grinning at Old Harry.

"Just as I thought," the older man repeated. "Old Harry

gets to know when somethin' special's happenin' up here, as the air gets crisp, like."

Sure enough, the others had noticed it now; a thin breeze had arrived, carrying with it a slightly prickly electrical charge. At the same time, everything around them seemed to become suddenly brighter, and a golden-white haze settled over the hillside.

"What's happening?" whispered Holly.

"What if I says, there's arrivin' a huge Homecomin' in the meadow later?" replied Old Harry jovially.

"I'd say you still talks weirdy," teased George giggling, and braced himself, ready to run if he got chased.

But Old Harry was in no mind or shape to be chasing anybody. He just shook his head slowly. "Them's a powerful cheeky family, an' that's the truth," he lamented to himself.

"That's great news about the party, thanks, Harry!" said Helen brightly. "I'm sorry that my, er…siblings are so cheeky with you. It just shows how relaxed you make them feel. Come on, let's go and watch the Homecoming."

"Rich that be, you apologising for them two young 'uns when I've had God knows how much cheek of yours along the years, my dear," chuntered Old Harry.

George wasn't quite sure now if he'd overstepped the mark and was looking down at his shoes as he walked along next to Old Harry.

"Always a first time for a Guide to be goin' on strike, you knows," Old Harry continued in his deep grumble, but he made sure to catch George's eye and wink at him to let him know he was only playing them at their own game.

George relaxed and he looked up again, smiling. "So where is the party, Harry, and when does it start?"

"This way!" called Helen, already half-skipping, half-running down the hill towards the meadow. "Race the lot of you!"

With Helen having thrown down the gauntlet, Holly and George took off immediately, desperate to overtake her. Old Harry strolled down the hill at a more dignified pace, still mumbling to himself. After a few yards, Helen slowed herself down imperceptibly to allow Holly and George to pelt past her. When they were a good fifty metres in front, and running at full tilt, she stopped abruptly and turned back towards Old Harry who was catching up slowly.

"I think *this* would be a good spot to watch the Homecoming from, don't you Harold?" she called up to him, indicating where she was standing, her eyes shining roguishly, as ever.

"As good as many an' better'n most, I reckons!" Old Harry agreed, sitting himself down next to Helen on the grassy slope.

"Hol-l-y! Geo-orge!" she called to her speeding siblings who by now had nearly reached the bottom of the slope. They heard her calling and skidded to a stop.

"We'll Watch From Up Here!" Helen shouted down through her cupped hands, "You Won't See A Thing From Down There!"

"If I didn't know you no better, I'd say you had a bit of a dark side in there someplace," noted Old Harry, tapping her forehead with his heavy forefinger as he arrived alongside her. "Mistreating them young 'uns like you does, it ain't right."

"Elder sister's prerogative, Harry, old chap," said Helen, a big smile across her pretty face. "Do you think it's something I should work on with my Guide...?" She just couldn't stop herself teasing Old Harry. Or practically anyone come to that.

"Next time I meets you back Downstairs, young scamp, if ever that day should come, I'll be throwin' a few challenges in your direction..."

"...an' that's the truth!" Helen finished his sentence for him, laughing gaily.

Old Harry glowered at her, but they both knew he was smiling inside.

Holly and George arrived back from the foot of the hill and flopped down next to Helen. Both were panting heavily, because, true to form they had had to race each other back up again too. Holly was stronger and faster, and had made sure she won by just a few feet, by slowing down to walk every few yards and waiting for George to almost catch her before taking off at a run again. So poor old George had had to run up the whole way to try and keep up, and now he was too exhausted to speak.

Holly was quite out of breath too, although she managed to gasp a few words. "You," she panted, "are… a… meany!"

Helen simply chuckled.

A few minutes later they had all settled down to watch the Homecoming party from the side of the hill. A large crowd of Souls was milling around on the steps in front of the palace. From the side of the hill they could hear the excited voices filling the air around them.

As she watched, Holly's eyes were drawn to a very, *very*, *very* tall Soul, surrounded with a white and gold aura, standing to one side of the crowd. It was so tall it looked like it was at least three times the height of the other Souls. It seemed as if it wasn't taking part in the Homecoming party, but was just keeping an eye on things.

"Who's that giant golden Soul?" she whispered to Helen,

transfixed by its height and dazzling glow.

"That, Holly," Helen whispered back, "is an Angel."

CHAPTER 16

The Angel And The Homecoming

"**A**n Angel!" cried George, who had regained his breath now. "Where? Where?! I want to see it! Show me, show me!"

"Look there, just to the right of the crowd. See him?" Helen pointed down the hill. "Angels often turn up just to make sure Homecomings go smoothly."

"Wooooo-ooowwww!! Yaaaaaa-aaaaaaayyyyy!!! Too coooo-ooolll!" George, apparently, seemed quite impressed.

Holly, on the other hand almost couldn't find any voice at all for a few moments. "An Angel!" she managed to gasp. "He's so tall...and so royal-looking...it looks like he's glittering, sort of ...sparkling..."

"How do you know it's a 'him'?" asked George, reasonably. "Maybe it's a 'her'!"

"Angels are neither him nor her, and – this'll confuse you - they are both, all at the same time," Helen explained, intriguingly.

George and Holly frowned quizzically at her.

"They have been chosen since the beginning of all time by all the forces of the Universe to be the highest power there is to look after beings everywhere. Not just on Earth, but up

Here too. They have never been anything else other than Angels, not humans, men or women, although we normally refer to an Angel as a 'him'."

"But no-one's talking to him!" George interrupted. "It's like everyone's pretending he's not even there!"

"No, Georgie, you're wrong about that. Look down there, what do you notice around the crowd?" Helen asked gently.

"Just a sort of goldy-whitey light," he answered.

"Just the same colour....as ...the Angel!" cried Holly, putting two and two together.

"There, you see! And that's how Angels talk to us," explained Helen. "They never talk in words. They send us thoughts wrapped up in that white and gold glow which is called an aura. On Earth, humans are surrounded by their own individual auras all the time too, although they usually aren't able to see them. Human auras glow in different colours and with different strengths according to the energy and attitude of that person at the time. An Angel's aura is always that perfect golden white colour which it uses to nourish everything it touches. It provides strength or happiness or wisdom or love... whatever is needed at any particular time."

"Can Angels help us with our challenges on Earth?" wondered Holly.

"Only in real emergencies, Hols. They can even come down and take a human form every now and then when they have to help sort out really difficult situations on Earth but they never stay any longer than is absolutely necessary," Helen replied.

As she said this, she couldn't resist the opportunity of turning to Old Harry, and fixing him with an impish stare. "All the *easy* challenges, the Guides can take care of," she taunted, biting over her bottom lip with her top teeth and scrunching her face up towards him, like a deranged rabbit.

Old Harry held her stare, his lips pursed, shaking his head slowly and grumbling something they couldn't catch about the misfortune of the just.

Helen was unfazed and stuck out her tongue at Old Harry and quickly turned back to her brother and sister. "Now, where was I before Harry rudely distracted me? Ah yes. Auras!" she giggled.

George was chuckling, seeing his sister getting away with cheeking her Guide like this. His mind filled with thoughts of how he used to love playing games with her back home. She was always making up new rules each time they played. Then he stared at the Angel and wondered what it must be like to never say any words out loud. He didn't think he'd be able to do it for very long and he was absolutely convinced

Holly could never do it even for two minutes.

"It looks like he's swallowed a light bulb!" he observed. "Loads of them! He's glowing from inside!"

"That's the aura of One Big Happiness," explained Helen. "It's the most perfect light there is. For Angels, it's actually what sustains them, their life-blood if you like. So right now, that Angel is talking to every one of those Souls at the same time, so they'll know exactly the right things to say and do to put their friend at ease when he arrives."

At that very moment the Angel raised its head and hands. It turned and looked directly towards where Holly and George were sitting on the hillside and a remarkable thing occurred.

"Look, Helen!" screeched Holly, "I'm glowing! I'm all sparkly and white and gold too!"

"Me too, me too!" cried George, excitedly.

Sure enough, all four of them were instantly surrounded with the Angel's golden-white aura. Holly and George started lifting up each of their limbs in turn like a human puppet show, examining each of their arms and legs as if they'd never seen them before. Which in a way, they hadn't. Not surrounded with an angelic aura like this. The air seemed to crackle with energy too, just like it had when George had grabbed Old Harry's finger earlier.

One Big Happiness. They'd heard the phrase several times since coming up Here and now they understood what it really felt like. They both felt as happy and warm and loved as they could ever remember feeling and instinctively they understood the Souls down at the Homecoming would be feeling exactly the same way.

Then, without any effort on their part, both Holly and George were lifted to their feet, in fact right *off* their feet. They found themselves suspended above the ground where they just floated, cocooned in the Angel's aura. They looked at each other in delight, and then over at Old Harry and Helen who were still seated on the grass, and looking at each other knowingly.

A calm, commanding voice entered both Holly's and George's heads simultaneously.

"In allowing this visit to you, George, and to you, Holly, the Soul Council has bestowed a precious and benign gift. It is an opportunity to which many aspire though few are sanctioned. What questions can I help you with?"

"Qu...Questions...?" croaked George, but was too overawed to continue and he dried up.

Holly took a deep breath. "I have a question," she began, and then she found her mouth was drying up too.

173

The Angel waited serenely.

Holly moistened her lips and cleared her throat. "Everyone up Here, all the Souls I mean, they seem so… well…so perfect, and, well, me and George, we sometimes do things wrong, and, you know…get into trouble. So we might not really…fit in up Here…?"

Her voice trailed off, and she was aware that the Angel probably had many better things to be doing than to listen to her talking about trivial things back at home.

The Angel, however, answered solemnly.

"Imperfection is unknowable in the Garden of Souls. Everything, everywhere is always as it is intended it should be."

"But what about down on Earth?" Holly asked, a frown of puzzlement creasing her forehead.

"Earth is but one part of the Garden of Souls, Child, as every other part of the Universe is too. No place exists that is not part of the Garden of Souls…"

"…yes but people always tell us that we have to be good on Earth before we will be allowed into Heaven though," persisted Holly, and then blushed bright red as she realised that she had just interrupted an Angel.

"The Garden of Souls is not a place one enters or leaves — it's a place where one just *is*... always,"

communicated the Angel, patiently, through its brilliant golden-white glow.

Holly's brain was struggling with the Angel's explanations. "I think I'm going to need a little time to think about all this," she said firmly. "I know you must be very busy with all these Souls to take care of, so we'd better let you get on with... Angel things." She recognised that her vocabulary was even more awestruck than she was and she opted for a polite finish. Even so, a slight stammer met her words as they left her mouth. "Th-Thank you for inviting me and George to v-v-visit," she managed.

"Your visit to us is likewise a gracious gift. In your guise as humans you valiantly choose the heroes' path to All-Knowingness. Your presence among us illuminates a beacon of courage, inspiring all Souls preparing to tread the complex and precarious learning path of Earthly incarnation. Your selfless journey is revered and applauded. May comprehension of the Interlife lead you to enlighten all those you touch. Learn in Happiness, Love and Peace,"

the Angel concluded.

George, feeling it was important that he was able to say he had talked with an Angel too, somehow inherited his sister's stammer, and could only manage "Um… th-thanks, er…y-you t-too," and experienced a very distinct disappointment that his contribution hadn't been more constructive.

The Angel lowered his hands and slowly turned back towards the crowd. After a few seconds the golden-white glow melted away from around the four hillside spectators. Holly and George were returned to the hillside with a bump and they both over-balanced and fell backwards. Neither could speak for a full thirty seconds.

"Woooo-oowww!" breathed George at length, his disappointment dissolved. "That was too cool!"

"There's not many visitors as can say they's been blessed by an Angel," Old Harry said slowly.

Helen was clearly impressed too. "George, Holly, I'm *so* proud of you!" she exclaimed, flinging her arms around both their necks at once, pushing them onto their backs and throwing herself on top of them for a group hug. "It's really rare that an Angel speaks to the visitors up Here," she told them. "So that makes you two very special indeed!"

And sure enough, Holly and George were indeed feeling very special right at that moment.

George spoke up first. "Only thing is…" he started.

"Only thing is...what, George?" asked Holly.

"Well, I know he's an Angel and everything, but...well, he used so many long words I'm not sure I completely understood everything he said!" confessed George, grinning embarrassedly.

Holly rolled her eyes upwards and groaned under her breath.

"'It's true, Master George, up Here them Angels has a habit of speakin' right posh," agreed Old Harry, winking at him.

"Just like you then, Harry!" said Holly, sweetly.

"Wise-cracker," growled Old Harry.

Helen laughed. "So what do you think you understood then?" she asked him.

"Well, I think he was saying that we are a good example to the Souls up Here who are thinking of going back down to earth..." replied George. "But why would *we* be a good example to *them*?" he asked.

"What do you think, Hols?" Helen tossed the question over to her sister.

"It sounded to me like he was saying that not many people get the chance to visit Soul School like we have. So...we should try to understand as much as we can so...we can help people back on Earth," Holly replied a little tentatively.

Helen and Old Harry exchanged approving glances, so Holly continued more confidently.

"And then, like George said, the Angel was saying that Souls up Here regard humans as heroes for choosing to learn on Earth, because life is much trickier down there than it is up Here."

"An' that's the truth!" confirmed Old Harry.

"Trickier yes, but don't forget it's up to you to make life on Earth a fabulous, fun experience too, in the same way as the Souls make their lives up Here," added Helen, wisely.

"Because we can choose our attitudes towards our challenges you mean…and how hard we're going to try to cope with them!" clarified Holly, looking straight at Old Harry and feeling just as wise.

"Exactly!" beamed her sister, proudly. "What else did you understand from the Angel?"

"Well…by having humans up Here visiting, might it prompt some Souls to stop dithering and get on with preparing their new Life-paths down on Earth?" Holly was half guessing at the last bit.

"Amen to that! Couldn't've put it no better meself," Old Harry congratulated her. "There's more'n a few Souls as does a bit too much ditherin' for my likes, time to time."

"You always were the slave-driver, Harold!" Helen was

teasing again. "But, being serious for a minute, we all know that life on Earth can be really fun and happy, but it can be tough and frustrating and often really painful and dangerous too. And that's why it's true that up Here we regard every Soul who is preparing to experience another life on Earth as a hero. And you're both definitely heroes...my specialest, bestest heroes!"

"Super Heroes!" beamed George, extending his arms in front of him and balling his hands into fists. "Up, up and away!"

"Such a...*boy*!" mocked Holly, airily.

"*My* Super Heroes!" laughed Helen, giving George a squishy bear hug so hard he complained he couldn't breathe.

"And ...what...do...you...mean..." asked George, one word at a time as he attempted to wriggle free from Helen's hug, "...exactly by 'coping with challenges'?"

"Aha! Holly will explain that to you one day, won't you Hols," smiled Helen. "But not today!"

"If *he* can understand a word *I* say," mocked Holly. Then turning to Helen, she said, "So the last time you were in Soul School you chose to learn from being my big sister, even though it was only for a short time."

"That's right, HolBol. That was one part I chose. Another was choosing to learn from being born to a mother that

179

wasn't ready to love me in the way a mother should. Sometimes our challenges don't take very long to meet fully, so when we've learnt the lessons we planned, we come back up Here immediately to review them.

"My challenges with you two and Mum and Dad were all about learning to create happiness, forgiveness and acceptance everywhere I could, even after being rejected myself. Old Harry helped me design a Life-path that could accomplish all that in around twenty years. So that's the life I experienced this time around and that's why I had to leave when I did to come back here, you see?"

"Yes," said Holly and George together, a little wistfully.

"So when the Angel talked about the Interlife, is that the same thing as Soul School then?" asked George.

"Pretty much, Georgie," replied Helen. "You'll hear some humans call it the Afterlife too, because they believe in having one life only, so the Afterlife for them is where their Soul goes *after* they have lived that one life on Earth. But we Souls also refer to it as the Interlife because we come and go to Earth many times. Just like right now, for instance, we are *in between* lives."

"So Souls can choose short lives or long lives then?" Holly pondered. "Or easy or difficult lives too? Some people seem to have terrible lives and really awful things happen to them."

"Yes that's true too," admitted Helen. "It's usually the more advanced Souls who deliberately choose the really difficult Life-paths, because they know that it is from the greatest hardships that the most powerful lessons are learnt."

"So they're not told to choose difficult lives because they did bad things in their previous lives then?" chipped in George.

"Not at all, Georgie," said Helen. "On Earth, people frequently might judge one another's actions, but they often overlook to judge themselves. You have to remember that no Soul up Here will *ever* judge any action by any human. We don't look at humans' actions on Earth as good or bad, we only consider them as a potential for learning and progress."

"How do you get to know everything...you know, about...everything?" George asked somewhat awkwardly, thinking he was not really sure if his question made much sense.

"No that's a very sensible question," said Helen, reading the uncertainty in his thought. "Do you remember the Angel mentioning 'All-Knowingness'?"

"I think I do..." reflected George.

"And you now know what is inside every human, don't you?"

"A Soul," replied George.

"And inside every Soul is…?"

"One Big Happiness?" guessed George, tentatively.

"Yes, that too! But also 'All-Knowingness'. Which means that when we need to know what to do about something difficult, we just have to remember where to look for the answer."

"So every answer to every question is already inside us. In our Soul, you mean?" George thought he understood. Almost.

"You're on the right track, Georgie! Super Hero strikes again!" Helen smiled at him.

And I remembered that all by myself! realised George, thinking maybe he had hit on another of the magpies' secrets. There weren't any magpies to be seen, however, but that didn't mean it couldn't be one of their secrets anyway. He felt like he was on a roll so he followed up with another question, "How do I find where my Soul *is*…exactly?"

"You just ask," answered Holly simply, remembering her Soul-searching conversation earlier with the R and D group.

George looked at her blankly.

Old Harry took up the baton. "Holly's right there, Master George, and up Here is a great place to be understandin' that piece of information an' all, whether or not she might later forget it Downstairs or not. An' believe me when I tells you that there's no small number of folks Downstairs as will take more'n just one lifetime to be finding it out too, so don't you be frettin' for the moment," he said.

Since there were no immediate questions from Holly or George on that subject he continued, "It ain't that I knows everythin' about everythin' no more'n you two might. What I does know is that the more I learns, the more questions I thinks up, just like as you be doin'. That there's the part for me as what's truly fun about learnin' – thinkin' up a bundle of triffic questions!

"Take your darlin' sister Helen here, (and I often gets to wishin' someone would…take her a long, long ways away I mean!)", he winked to George as he said this. "There be still Life Lessons galore in front of her to be learnin', an' Life Choices by the boatload an' all. We has precious little ideas yet, the both of us, as to what she'll be up to next time around, nor where, nor when neither, but what I can guarantee you all is, she'll not stop askin' them triffic questions. Like as I said before, that there's the part as what's truly fun about learnin'."

"My teacher at school tells us off for asking too many questions," piped up Holly.

"Teachers is good folk, an' they does the best they can,

Miss Holly. My rule is: If he be a triffic question, then he be worth lettin' out," said Old Harry. "An'if he ain't, best keep him inside."

"How do we know if it 'be' a 'triffic' question, or not though?" persisted Holly, trying to stop the corners of her mouth from curling up into a give-away smile.

Old Harry was long enough in the tooth to know when his leg was being pulled.

"Here's a clue, me duck. That question..." he put on a stern face at Holly, "...was most definitely *un*-triffic."

"Ah! Right!" said Holly, her rascally smile making the most of its long-awaited liberty.

After a few moments they all turned their eyes back to the happy Homecoming crowd.

Over to the left, Helen pointed out a large opening in the side of the hill opposite and George and Holly could just make out an old, quite tall, dark haired man, emerging from it, making his way towards the crowd up on the steps. Although he had only just arrived, he seemed to know already exactly where he was, and why he was here. He wasn't close enough to the crowd to make out any faces yet and he looked slightly anxious, wondering if he was going to know anyone as he neared the expectant crowd.

"Now watch this!" cried Helen, and just as she spoke the

crowd suddenly all started cheering and clapping and laughing. Now he was close enough, the man recognised some familiar faces and some memorable, cherished voices. His face broke into the widest smile Holly thought you could ever fit onto one face. The man started running the last few steps towards the crowd and then disappeared from sight as he was swept up into a sea of hugs and smiles and kisses and happy shouts.

"Coming back here for a Homecoming with all your Soul friends and loved ones is just One Big Happiness!" beamed Helen, who seemed to be every bit as happy as the crowd on the steps, even though she didn't know any of them.

"That's exactly what it was like for me when I came back again last year. Can you see now why you don't have to be sad? There are so many of our Soul friends and family up Here to play with and to look after us. So just you be happy for me when you go back down to Earth! That's an order! And you can tell everybody else I said so too!" she said, laughing.

The happy hum from the Homecoming party was becoming louder and louder as the old man recognised more and more of the Souls who had turned up to welcome him back. Holly watched the golden-white glow of One Big Happiness surrounding the whole crowd, and she noticed the

Angel had left the steps from where he had been watching and was now nowhere to be seen.

"He's done his job for now," Old Harry observed.

Holly and George had turned to face the Homecoming party crowd and were staring intently at the delighted Soul crowd. Old Harry said he'd take them down and introduce them to the party-goers, but George, and even Holly this time, felt there were a few too many new Souls to be meeting all at once. In the end they decided to watch a little longer from the hillside. Old Harry said he had to go and get some work done, and left the three of them to it, but only after promising faithfully to catch them later, before they left to go "Downstairs" again.

"That Homecoming party will go on for hours yet," said Helen. "And those aura colours will always remind you of what being happy and being loved really feel like. The next few times you feel a bit confused about what to do, I'll send you both a little golden-white thought-signal, so look out for it. Then you'll know what to do in no time, you'll see."

George announced he still felt a bit 'crackly' from the 'talk' with the Angel and he lay on his front on the grassy hillside, surrounded by crocuses and daisies. He propped himself up on his elbows, holding his chin in both hands, lost in his thoughts.

Old Harry's mad phrases made him chuckle to himself –
there was certainly a 'bundle of triffic questions' taking
shape in his head.

CHAPTER 17

The Learning Playground

"**A** penny for your thoughts, Georgie," Helen sensed George wanted to talk.

George looked up, but said nothing.

"You OK?" she enquired.

"Um...yes, fine, I think," replied George. "It's just, well...I was just thinking about all those people, those *Souls*," he corrected himself, "those Souls at the Homecoming. It's like...it's like they are so *alive*! Just like you and Harry are too, obviously. Even though you're all... well, supposed to be dead! And the man who arrived too, he seemed so *alive* too, didn't he?"

"We're all very alive indeed up Here!" agreed Helen, smiling.

"Yes, but...so...if everyone really is alive up Here, then that means you can't be...completely dead, doesn't it?" he asked, trying desperately to work out what on earth he was getting at as he talked.

"Du-ur!" Holly jeered, pulling a simpleton's face and placing her right forefinger against her chin.

"No, Hols, let him work it through," said Helen gently, "I think I see where he's going with this."

George pulled a face back at Holly.

"What I mean is, I know you must all have died on Earth to be able to come up Here, but…" he paused, and then it came to him, "…up Here, it's like you've never stopped being alive!"

"That's a wonderful observation, George," said Helen. "And so…?"

George knew he was on to something and carried on excitedly, "…So if we *are* alive all the time, up Here, as Souls…then dying down there can't *really* exist, can it? And if dying didn't exist, then there'd be no point being afraid of it, would there?"

"You are so, so wise for someone who is only seven!" said Helen, proudly, stooping to put her arms around his neck.

"Nearly ten!" sang George automatically, who was actually feeling very wise indeed for having worked all of this out.

"But dying *does* exist!" countered Holly, forcefully. "Humans *do* die, it's a fact! *You*...died," she trailed off, wishing she didn't have to say those words to her sister. "And Mum and Dad sprinkled your ashes round the Poppy Tree!"

"Yes, that's all true, Hols. But think for a moment; at

what point do humans die?" challenged Helen, softly. "Cast your mind back to the Hall with the Green Books…"

Holly thought hard. "When they've finished the experiences they planned for themselves, I suppose," she replied. "Or when they had gone as far as they could with meeting all their challenges? Or both?" She hoped she was on the right track.

"Right so far…" Helen started to confirm.

"But only the 'human bit' really dies, doesn't it?" George chipped in. "'Cos the 'Soul bit' stays alive and comes straight up Here for a Homecoming and then back to Soul School. That's right isn't it, Hels?"

"Are you calling me a 'Soul bit'?!" laughed Helen. Then, imitating Old Harry's gruff voice, she said to Holly, "That's a powerful bright brother you's got there, young Missy!"

George grinned cheerfully. "So that's why you said death on Earth is the beginning, not the end…?" he summarised, tentatively.

"Exactly! Or *another beginning* to be more precise. *Now* you are starting to see what Soul School is really all about!" confirmed Helen. "What people on Earth see as 'dying,' we Souls up Here see simply as a sort of '*learning pause*.' In other words, dying is simply a time when Souls can take a much-deserved break from their challenging Life-paths on

Earth. It's a time for coming back up to Soul School for a progress check and a well-earned rest!"

"A learning pause..." repeated George. "You mean it's just like having playtime between lessons at school?"

"Well, almost," agreed Helen. "Except that up Here in Soul School everyone enjoys learning so much that the learning itself feels like playtime for us too. That's what Souls love to do best of all, remember - learn in a playful way!"

"So...Soul School is nothing but one huge, fun, learning playground!" announced Holly, authoritatively.

"That's exactly what it is!" agreed Helen. "One huge, fun, learning playground! I can't think of a better way to describe it myself!"

They all fell silent for some minutes, thinking their own thoughts. Their eyes returned to the Homecoming party crowd. It had moved away from the School steps now, and the revellers had reached the vast park with the lake and fountains and waterfalls where, Helen had told them, they would keep partying for hours and hours.

It was Helen who broke the silence.

"Right, you two, now we've got to start thinking about getting you back to Mum and Dad, because Tik and Rilke will be waiting to take you home again and I've got an R and

D session later," she said firmly. She knew they'd want to stay longer with her but she felt they'd seen and learnt enough, so it was the right time to go.

She led them down past the impressive, timeless stone steps in front of the palace. Just before they reached the path leading to the meadow, they stopped to look up at the enormous stone and marble and glass buildings for the last time. They had been so wrapped up in the Homecoming happiness that she hadn't noticed another group of Souls standing together near the top step. Holly tugged at her sister's sleeve and Helen stopped and turned to see what she wanted.

"Those Souls…" began Holly, "they don't seem nearly as happy as the others. Are they sad about something?"

"Holly this is Home, remember! Sadness doesn't exist up Here at all!" Helen reminded her, smiling fondly. "No, those Souls are just preparing to say goodbye to a Soul Friend who will be going back down to Earth to start her next Life-path. Just like the Angel said, they know all about the ups and downs of living on Earth and how tricky it can be. After all, by this stage, their Soul Friend will have chosen all the major learning points that she is going to experience on Earth, so it's normal that she is a little apprehensive.

"What she'll be preparing to do now, is to take one last,

long look at all the maps and charts of places and people on Earth so she can put the finishing touches to her own Chart."

"What do you mean by a Chart?" asked Holly.

"A Chart is a plan every Soul writes for itself with the help of its Guides, outlining all the options it can encounter down on Earth. Souls choose what they believe would be the most perfect environment for them to be born into and to grow up in, and to face their challenges and life lessons.

"For example, they choose which parents they will be born to, which countries, and cities and neighbourhoods they will live in, what their hobbies and interests will be, what they are going to look like, who their brothers and sisters will be…"

"Ah, that explains something," interrupted George. "So you're saying Holly *chose* to be a Pongy, Koala-faced Twitbrain…"

Holly grabbed at his ear, but George was too quick and ducked easily under her flailing arm.

Helen laughed, "Don't forget Holly chose you too, Georgie."

"Why I would ever choose to experience living with a Whiffy, Snotty Stick Insect is beyond me!" Holly retorted.

"'Cos you've got great taste, Whale Head," countered George, quick as a flash.

"Enough zonking you two," giggled Helen. "Now let me finish explaining this to you because it's a lot to take in. When this Soul has finished with the maps and charts, her Soul Friends will spend a little time together planning how and when they might show up in each other's Life-paths.

"They may decide to play a big part in her Life-path or to just appear for a few minutes at seemingly completely random times. We call those appearances 'interventions'. Whatever the length of the intervention they decide on, those interventions are designed to provide just the right learning for that particular moment in her life. However, because the person will have completely forgotten what she wrote into her Chart while she was up Here, she can only receive the learning if she chooses to be open to it at that same moment. And that depends on the frame of mind she chooses towards learning at any given stage of her life. Much of the time, people don't realise straight away why someone or something has crossed through their lives and brought them a useful insight. However, when they reflect later, in the right frame of mind, they can know that that moment was entirely in synch with their Chart, and their life is unfolding exactly as they planned it."

"Does that mean that *everything* that happens to us on Earth is already planned? Because that means it wouldn't matter how we coped with anything if things were going to happen anyway!" reasoned Holly.

"Good question, Hols, and the answer is no, not *everything* is planned, just the more important outlines, choices and probabilities. The rest is up to us and our freewill to fill in the gaps."

"What's freewill?" asked George.

"Freewill means we have freedom to choose which path to take." answered his sister.

"Even if it's the wrong one?" persisted George.

"Well, this is always a bit tricky to understand first off, Georgie, but from a Soul's point of view there is no wrong or right path – there is only a *learning opportunity*," explained Helen. "Humans decide things are right or wrong depending on how they are interpreting the Chart they have written for themselves. Souls simply accept that everything is as it should be, just like the Angel told you. Souls are just looking to experience things to experience what they feel like. Does that make any sense to you at all?"

"Um…" replied George, wishing he could say yes, but really feeling hopelessly lost.

"Don't worry, Porge, there are some things that you don't need to fully understand on this visit, and that bit is definitely one of those. All in good time," smiled Helen.

"Do you think she has planned a very difficult life?" asked Holly, changing the subject, because, truth be told, she was feeling a bit lost too. "Her friends look very nervous."

"I have no idea, Hols, but you needn't worry that she won't be taken care of. Remember, the more advanced the Soul is, the tougher the Charts they like to write for themselves, and the more they will be well watched over. Those Soul Friends up there too, they are not nervous so much; they love their friend and they will know what she has written into her Chart, and how tough or otherwise it may be, so they are just concerned about her, that's all."

"Then why don't they just keep her up Here a bit longer? Maybe she could do some more studying in Soul School?" asked George, who didn't really see why anyone would want to leave a place where they were always happy and loved.

"That's the whole point. It's because they love her that they have to let her go, Georgie. They know that sometimes, meeting some difficult challenges and making some big mistakes is the best way to learn in the long run," Helen explained. "Remember, life on Earth is about *coping* with experiences in a strong way. They are concerned but also excited for her and they trust her to make the best job she can of the difficult Life-path she's chosen."

"I still don't understand...yet," said George.

"OK, let me think how I can explain it in a different way," said Helen, patiently. "Right, imagine Mum and Dad do everything they can to protect you while you're growing up, and they never even let you go out of the house in case something might happen to you. Imagine they watched over you *all the time*," Helen said. "How would you feel?"

"I'd probably feel a bit like being a parrot in a cage. I might feel protected but I think I would be really bored too," replied George.

"Knowing you, I'd say you definitely would!" agreed Helen. "So, for example, you would never get to climb up the Poppy Tree in the garden, would you?"

"But they let me climb the tree since I was four!" George said.

"That's right, and to begin with, Dad or I would always climb with you, wouldn't we, to make sure you didn't fall out, and to show you where to hold on to," Helen reminded him. "And when you were five or six and a bit stronger and taller, and you'd got used to it, they let you climb it all by yourself, didn't they?"

"Yes, and I used to spend hours up there, with my soldiers," George grinned as he remembered all the games he used to make up. "But they always told me not to go too high into the smaller branches near the top, so I'd stay safe."

"That's right, you loved being in that tree," recalled Helen. "But it was hard for Mum and Dad to let you climb up all by yourself the first few times. You could easily have fallen out or hurt yourself, but because they love you and want you to learn to have confidence in yourself, they needed to let you climb it all by yourself too, without any help."

"I never fell out though did I?" said George.

"No you didn't," agreed Helen. "But we were always watching out for you through the kitchen window, just in case something happened."

"I never knew that!" cried George.

"Watch-ee! Watch-ee! Baby in the Tree-ee!" sang Holly.

"I'd keep quiet if I were you, Hols," warned Helen, grinning, "Mum *still* watches you up there and you're *twelve*!!"

"Ha!" cried George, gleefully. "Mum-my Watch-ee, Ba-bee, Mon-kee!"

"Well, I never saw anyone watching me," pouted Holly, her hands on her hips.

"My point exactly. Just because we don't always notice people, who are watching out for us, or notice Soul interventions, for that matter, doesn't mean they're not there!" Helen put her arms around them both and hugged them. To illustrate her point she gestured up at the small crowd on the steps again.

"Look over there. All those Souls will be watching out for their friend when she has gone down again to Earth, just like we used to watch over you through the kitchen window. So if things ever get really tough for her, they'll be watching out for her even though she won't see them. They'll know what to do to make sure she experiences the lessons in the right way."

"Can we talk to her?" asked George. "You know…ask her about her Life-path and the things she's chosen to do?"

"'Fraid not, Georgie," said Helen. "That's personal to her and her Soul Family. But who knows, your Life-paths might cross on Earth one day. You can ask her what you like then."

"But how will I recognise her!" asked George. "How will I know where she's going to live?"

"That, my specialest little bruv, is one of the best things about being on Earth, in my opinion. On Earth, we never know quite why we are drawn towards certain people, or where we might meet someone important, or what they might be able to teach us. And, chances are, if you make a friend that you feel really comfortable with, it may be because you've already met that Soul in another Life-path."

"So that's what Old Harry meant when he said strangers

are just friends that we haven't met yet," said Holly.

"He did, didn't he, well remembered!" smiled Helen.

"He actually said strangers are... kif...kinfa...what was that word he used, the one you said means 'family'?" asked George.

"'Kinfolk,'" Helen reminded him.

"That's it. He actually said strangers are just kinfolk we haven't met yet!" recalled George.

"Soul Friends, Soul Family – all much the same thing up Here," said Helen. "Old Harry will tell you that up Here, Souls are all part of one big family, but obviously some have a bigger influence on our learning than others. We can't possibly meet every Soul there is, nor do we need to because there is so much to learn from those who are charted to cross our path naturally.

"As Harry says, we stick with the Souls we learn from best, from one life to the next, and anytime we need a particular new learning we'll always come across the right Soul to teach us, because we've charted it already. That's how it works up Here. But remember, George, up Here *all* Souls are *always* going to be friendly when you talk to them. On Earth, people might have their own reasons for not being so well-intentioned, so you have to be more careful and selective whom you choose to talk to."

Holly gave George one of her 'long-hard-and meaningful' looks as Helen said that.

"That's why when you meet someone that interests you on Earth, for whatever reason, you should decide if it feels right to talk to them. If it does, then always start by asking them lots of questions. Humans especially love to be asked about themselves. Try it, you'll make loads of friends that way and learn lots of new things too!"

"You always made tons of friends, wherever you went," acknowledged Holly.

"I rest my case!" beamed Helen.

They all sat in silence for a few moments gathering their thoughts.

Then George piped up. "Are there Souls watching over me too, you know, down on Earth…?"

"Course there are, George! All the time," confirmed Helen. "Holly's Guide is called Sophie and…

"Remember the woman we saw that made us decide to climb up to the magpies' nest?" interrupted Holly, quickly. "That was Sophie, my Guide, that was."

"…and your Guide is called Kati."

"Katie?" echoed George.

"No, not 'Katie', George – it's pronounced 'Kati' - rhymes with Fatty!" Helen poked him playfully in his belly.

"She was born into a German family in her last life on Earth."

"But I can't speak German," protested George. "How will I know what she says?"

"She speaks to you in Soul Speak," answered Helen, grinning. "All Guides do. People just hear them in their own language. Sophie and Kati are both around anytime you have questions. And of course, I'll be keeping an eye on you always, too."

"Hel...?" Holly spoke up in a small voice.

"What's up, HolBol?"

"Well, you just made me think of something," said Holly, feeling a little gawky. "Mum told me that George used to play with an imaginary cat till he was about three."

"Yeah, so? She told me that too, but I was only *three*!" George retorted defensively.

"No...but...Georgie, what I'm saying is that you used to talk to it all the time, and you used to call it 'Catty'. Whenever you wanted to talk in your baby talk you would call out 'Catty! Catty!'"

"So he did!" remembered Helen, "I'd forgotten all about that."

"So what, anyway?" frowned George, thinking they were playing another joke on him that he couldn't understand.

"No, George, listen! Catty. Kati. Kati. Catty. It's the same word! The same name I mean. Maybe you were talking to your Guide, not an imaginary cat like Mum thought?"

"Maybe I was…?" wondered George, trying to remember the last time he'd talked to 'Catty'.

"It's quite probable, in fact, now you mention it, Hols," said Helen. "Just like Harry said, it's not unusual for children to hold onto a few memories from Soul School in their early years, but it usually fades away quite quickly. In your case, three years, Georgie Porge!"

"I'm going to start talking to her again when I get back," announced George.

"And I'm going to talk to Sophie," announced Holly, not to be outdone.

"You both do that," smiled Helen.

CHAPTER 18

Jody Makes An Impression

A t that moment Old Harry floated in, and just behind him was another youngish Soul, who looked like he was only about fifteen. Quite tasty actually, thought Holly.

Helen read her mind and winked at her.

Holly blushed bright red.

Jody read her mind too and winked at Helen.

Holly blushed bright scarlet and turned away.

"Now then, now then, what has my young heroes been playin' at while I's been hard at work?" Old Harry asked, amiably. "Seein' as how I's practically an expert in that kite-flyin' malarkey nowadays…"

"Kite-surfing!" George corrected him jumping to his feet and running towards the newcomer. "Hi, Jody!" he beamed, "Holly, this is Jody, he's my friend from the lake, and we went…"

"Yes, Georgie, I think you can spare us all the details, this time around," said Helen quickly. "Hello again, Jody, this is my sister, Holly."

"Hey, Holly," said Jody, in a pleasant, chatty voice, holding out his hand. Holly shook it, looking at his wispy blue goatee. She was too embarrassed to say anything since he'd read her thoughts earlier. She strained to make her mind go blank so he couldn't read her thoughts *now*.

"…oh aye, kite-*surfin'*. That be right," Old Harry carried on regardless. "So I finds me way over to the lake an' gets talkin' to young Jody here, an' I gets to tellin' him about two young heroes I has had the privilege of meetin' - them as who'd been chattin' with an Angel, only a little while back," he informed them in his wonderful, convoluted manner.

"I hear you're both off soon," said Jody.

"Yeah, Helen says the magpies are waiting in the meadow to take us home, but we could go quickly back to the lake and I could show them how we do kite-surfing, and…" George was revving up again.

"George…!" warned Helen, wagging her finger at him.

"No but it would just be *really* quick and you could all have a go and …"

"George! Stop! Enough!" ordered Helen, smiling at his energy. "The lake is in *that* direction," she pointed behind her, "and the meadow is in *this* direction," she pointed in front. "And *this* direction is thé only direction we're going in right now!"

"But…!"

"Come *ON*, George! We can't keep Rilke and Tik

waiting," chimed in Holly, bossily. Just a teeny bit of her felt it needed to show Jody how big sisters took control of little brothers.

"OK.OK. I was only saying, that's all." grumbled George.

"Right, well now you've *said*," established Holly walking purposefully forwards. The truth, she had little enthusiasm for leaving either, but she knew it was inevitable.

"Ah well, George, what can we men do when the women have made up their minds, eh?" shrugged Jody, holding his palms face up to the sky and glancing sideways at Holly as he spoke.

Holly went red as a raspberry once again.

"Anyway," Jody continued. "It takes a while to really master that kite-board. There's a lot to learn before you get to where it's really fun *and* safe too. Took me years to learn it. I started when I was about eight."

"So it's not too difficult?" asked George, trudging as slowly as he could towards the meadow. "I mean, too difficult for someone who's nearly ten…?"

Holly opened her mouth to contradict her brother, but Old Harry caught her eye and winked at her. She held her tongue, but it was an effort and she pursed her lips, narrowed her eyes and shook her head, slowly and pointedly, from side to side.

"Hey, mate, nothing's too difficult if you really <u>want</u> to do it!" Jody said brightly. "Just don't worry about making mistakes and all that. When you're learning something new, and you're finding it difficult, the most important thing to do is ...well... to just do *something*!"

"The most important thing to do is to do something?" queried George. "Sounds weirdy! You mean, if I don't do *something*, I can't make any mistakes..."

"...and if you never make any mistakes...?" Jody steered...

"...then...I can't really learn very much, can I?!" George immediately understood where Jody was leading and he puffed up his chest and strutted around like a proud peacock.

Holly rolled her eyes, although her brother's new friend was chuckling at his antics.

"Hole in one, buddy!" beamed Jody, putting his arm across George's shoulders. "The more things you do, the more mistakes you might make, but it all makes more things to learn from too!"

"Even if the things I do aren't very difficult?" asked George.

"Sure, there's loads you can learn from them too." Jody clapped him on the back, encouragingly.

"And if they are difficult, like kite-surfing is, I can still do them, I just have to *believe* I can," George reflected, already thinking about telling Dad he was going to be a World Champion kite-surfer.

"That, buddy," grinned Jody, "is the perfect way to look at it! And you want to know one more thing?" he asked.

George looked up at him expectantly. "Tell me."

"Ten's about the right age to start kite-surfing," Jody told him, "provided you're a really good swimmer too."

George was quite a good swimmer already but he felt a little deflated when Jody mentioned the age part, and Holly, who had been pretending not be interested, but really had been keeping tabs on the whole conversation, smirked to herself.

Then Jody leaned down close to George's head.

"But…" he said, as he cupped his hands around George's ear and whispered through them so only George could hear, "World Champions probably start about seven!"

George's face lit up. Jody offered him a high five and George leapt up and slapped it.

As soon as she could, Holly pulled George to one side by his arm. "What did he say?" she asked tersely.

"Secret! Secret! Not for Girly Tomato Cheek Heads!" George called back snootily to his sister whose face just wouldn't stop blushing. He wrenched his arm free and ran to join the others who were nearing the meadow.

As they were about to enter the magical meadow for the final time they turned together to take a last look at this extraordinary place they had been granted permission to visit. The imperial stone and marble halls and the crystal towers stretched into the distance as far as they could see. They took a lingering look at the ornamental gardens and fountains, the park in the distance with the lake and the statues and the waterfall. Now they had come to know it so much better, it did indeed feel like a land they belonged to and they both instinctively understood why Souls called it Home.

"Do you have any last questions before you go?" asked Helen, acutely aware of Holly and George's reluctance to leave.

"Yes, I do!" cried George! "Can I go kite-surfing just one more little time with Jody?" he pleaded.

Me too! wished Holly to herself, and then blushed beetroot again, remembering how transparent her thoughts were in this company.

"Next question!" laughed Helen, ruffling George's hair with her fingers.

"Nice try, buddy," smiled Jody. "You go for it Downstairs, OK?"

"I will," said George, firmly.

CHAPTER 19

Triffic Questions

"I've got a question," started Holly, some minutes later. "I think it might even be a 'triffic' one!" she prepared them all, trying to lighten her mood by teasing Old Harry.

"Go on, Hols" encouraged Helen.

Holly let out a long, deep breath while she collected her thoughts together.

"Well," she began, concentrating hard. "When I'm back down on Earth again, whatever I remember about Soul School and everything that happens up Here...well no-one's going to believe me when I tell them are they? I mean, most people on Earth don't really believe in having several lives, or that we plan the one we're living in Soul School before we're even born.

"And that's even assuming I remember anything at all, because you said, Harry, that I'm going to forget how I learnt what I do remember, and I might not even believe any of it myself anyway, 'cos I'll be only human again won't I...?"

She stopped short, a little downcast, realising everything was coming out all wrong. She'd thought she had her question all sorted before she started and it didn't help either that she was talking nonsense with you-know-who present.

Old Harry took on the task of unravelling Holly's question. The rest of them took on the task of unravelling Old Harry's vocabulary.

"Young Miss Holly, I crowns you undisputed Queen of Triffic Questions," he declared, chortling roundly. "That there's not only a Triffic Question, it's a Humdingin'ly Triffic Question! Why, there must be nigh on an 'undred questions all rolled into one, sure as bubble is squeak!"

Despite his making fun of her, Holly had come to love the way Old Harry joined in their mischief, and she didn't mind him pulling her leg any more, even in front of The Gorgeous Goatee-d One. She knew she could trust him. After all, Helen had trusted him for centuries, so she prepared to listen carefully to what he was about to tell her.

"Simple fact is," Old Harry continued, "you and Master George comin' visitin' Upstairs and knowin' what you now knows, ain't about no-one else but you two. It ain't no mind whether folks Downstairs believes you or doesn't. Most folks Downstairs is comfortable enough believin' there be some sort of livin' after dyin' anyways. It's just how that livin' takes shape they can't agree on. Some believes they'll be comin' back and some doesn't. That's up to them and you

214

can't be doin' their thinkin' for 'em, nor should you.

"As to whether you remembers or you doesn't what you's seen up Here, it ain't no mind there neither. Nor whether you chooses to believe it was all a dream. It's plain to see you has a powerful spirit, young Holly, and them folks as what gets to meet you Downstairs is going to be the lucky ones, take my words as gospel. You has chose a right special Life-path Downstairs, even as you doesn't know it rightly yet, so my guess be that your Soul'll be lookin' for ways to be remindin' you of more'n a large part of what you has seen and learned up Here, me duck. Already you's storin' it all away for when you needs to be usin' it. An' use it you most certainly shall.

"More 'n' likely you'll lose count of the times you finds yourself misunderstood tryin' to explain to folks how the world makes sense to you. Truth is, none of that matters, long as you knows where *you's* goin' with it and why. Life Downstairs can be right simple if you looks at it this way: Understand your motivation, understand everythin'."

Helen, who had been giggling behind her hands, started clapping and whooping.

"Wooo Woooo! Bravo, Harold!" she teased. "That must be the longest you've ever spoken uninterrupted. Sit down you must be exhausted!"

215

Old Harry narrowed his eyes and looked sideways at her without turning his head, then back at Holly. He paused, "So, how's I doin' with that Humdinger Question of yours?"

"You're not even halfway through it yet!" chided Helen, enjoying herself.

"You be not doin' bad, Master Harry," Holly shot back, joining in with Helen's impertinence.

"Yep, there be that spirit I noted, that be it right there!" Old Harry couldn't help chuckling away at the banter, clearly enjoying himself too. "An' I ain't finished yet neither!

"Now then, as to whether *you* ends up believin' what you's seen and learned up Here. That there's a tricky one an' I'll share you why I thinks so. Truth is, once you's livin' Downstairs, one part of you'll want to accept it, another part'll want to reject it. There's always one side in humans that pushes while another side pulls. That's their nature. It ain't easy for folks Downstairs to accept what they can't see and can't prove so most folks'll choose to reject it, 'cos life'll be much more straightforward for 'em that way."

"You can't blame people for looking for an easy life though, can you?" asked Holly, reasonably.

"Indeed you can't, young Holly, indeed you can't. And that be the whole nature of challenges, like we's talked about before. There's a lot to be said for choosin' the easy life, and doin' what we's always done. There's some learnin' in there too, truth be told. But the real learnin' comes when we's bold enough to try somethin' when we hasn't a clue how it's goin' to turn out."

"How do we know what we're going to learn then, if we don't know what we're doing?" persisted Holly.

"We doesn't, Missy. Like I says, not a clue. That there's the whole point. Let me ask you in return, what does we learn by doin' what we already knows about, day in day out?"

"Well. The more we do something we know, the better we understand it, so it feels right..." reflected Holly.

"Aha! So if you is *right* doin' what you understands an' you meets people who understands diff'rent things to you, do that make them *wrong*?" asked Old Harry, clearly in his stride now.

Helen noticed a glint of amusement in his eyes as he jousted words with her young sister.

"Not wrong...necessarily," Holly was floundering slightly, "just... different, that's all..."

"Both wrong? Both right?"

"No, neither, both different that's all!" said Holly exasperated. "There can be more than one way to do

217

something, you know."

"Oh I believes that, indeed I does. So is you inclined to agree that if we accepts that somethin' diff'rent from what we *does* might be right, then somethin' diff'rent from what we *believes* might be right an' all?"

Holly's inquisitive instinct was to counter with another quick-fire question, but on this occasion although she opened her mouth to speak, no words came out. She fell silent, looking straight at Old Harry, a grouchy, but pensive expression clouding her face.

Old Harry met her gaze evenly, savouring the silence.

After a few seconds, Holly couldn't stand the pause any longer and stuck her tongue out at Old Harry, shaking her head at him as she did so.

Old Harry laughed. "It's true, it can be a tricky thing to understand," he conceded, graciously. "So what you does know, now as you's visiting Upstairs Here with us, is that folks Downstairs accepts or rejects diff'rent beliefs dependin' on the Life Choices they's undertook in Soul School. The same ol' problem bein' that they can't remember ever bein' at Soul School, of course.

"Belief without proof is a powerful tough Life-path challenge even for *advanced* Souls to be choosin', so it stands to reason it be a good way too tough for most others too. Yep, decidin' whether to believe in this 'ere Interlife, or not believe, many folks Downstairs finds it too challenging one way or the other and they ends up believin' somewhere in between. An' that means when they comes back Upstairs they's got it all to work on afresh. That's why it can take a number of lifetimes to sort it for some of 'em."

He paused again to let his words sink in.

"So what be the message of that little story then, d'you think?" he asked Holly, after a few moments.

"Well, it sounds like the opposite of when people say they have to see it to believe it," began Holly. "It's like you said - humans need to have proof of something *before* they can accept it..."

"Indeed I did," encouraged Old Harry, "go on..."

"So...a different way would be if life worked the other way round – 'believe it to see it,' " resumed Holly, concentrating hard. "You're saying that people might understand things better if they chose to believe in them *first*, in order that they can see them *later*," she concluded logically, although it sounded a little strange to hear herself say it.

"'Xactly right, me duck, 'xactly right!" confirmed Old Harry. "That be what we means by 'having faith' - believin' things *before* we sees them, *before* we has proof, like. An' it takes a hero-brave human to meet an' pass that partic'lar 'faith-challenge' Downstairs, Miss Holly, an' that's the truth!"

Holly nodded slowly, concentrating hard.

"An' one last thing for me to be sharin' you before you departs though, an' I means for you both to hear fair and true. That's you an' all, Master George."

George's ears pricked up. He'd been finding Old Harry's summary pretty hard going, and although he'd been doing his best to follow over the last few minutes, in truth his mind had been wandering back to kite-surfing and swimming and beach volleyball. He looked up sharply as he heard his name mentioned, feeling a little guilty, and did his best to put an earnest learning expression on his face.

"Jokin' aside now. Fact be, I knows you two is goin' to be right triffic leaders this Life-path Downstairs. You wants to know how I knows?"

They nodded.

"It be 'cos you not only knows triffic questions to be askin', you ain't afraid to be askin' 'em. An' once you's asked 'em, you listens right powerful back before you acts. Leaders does that, an' outstandin' leaders you most definitely be, the both of you.

"Leadin' folks ain't about guidin' others to follow, it's

about guidin' others to lead, an' it's rare that I's met two young Souls more suited to be understandin' how to do just that. I'm right proud to know the both of you."

Both Holly and George glowed with the sincerity of Old Harry's tribute. They felt almost the same way they had when the Angel had surrounded them with his golden-white aura. One Big Happiness! It was a beautiful feeling with which to end their visit, and both of them silently admitted to themselves that they were, at last, ready to go home.

Downstairs home. Earth home. The place where a lifetime of tricky challenges and precarious situations awaits 'Hero-brave Humans' as Old Harry calls them.

But also a lifetime of fun, amazement and joy. All that hero-brave humans needed to remember was to choose the right attitudes. The way Old Harry told it, it did indeed seem very simple.

CHAPTER 20

The Send-Off

Beautiful, silky butterflies of all sizes and colours fluttered everywhere as they re-entered the magical meadow. Rilke and Tik were waiting patiently in the middle, either side of the old nest. And of course, Wakke, Ponke, Teleka and Quok had turned up for the Send-off party, cackling animatedly and goading each other into arguments.

Dazzling colours greeted them every step of the way; birds, dragonflies, caterpillars, flowers, shrubs, the skies and even the grass seemed to radiate colours of every hue imaginable. Inevitably, everything was surrounded by the same hazy golden-white aura.

Souls started arriving from every direction. Zack and Zoe drifted in, followed soon after by Ramon and Morgan having finished their R and D session. Asif and Charlie and a dozen other volleyball-playing Souls in beach shorts and bikinis turned up. Several Souls whom Holly thought she recognised from the Library and dozens more whom she didn't, floated into the meadow. Sarah and Jayminee from the R and D class arrived, out of breath.

"Sorry, sorry, sorry!" they said. "We got caught up in an

extra long class. So glad we caught you before you left, so happy to meet you. Good luck! Good bye!"

Everyone crowded round and said their goodbyes, hugged them tightly and gave them messages of goodwill. Holly even let Jody give her a hug although she kept her own hands by her sides. It wouldn't do to be too forward, she told herself, blushing to the roots of her hair all the while.

Two elderly ladies walked slowly towards them. Holly's mouth dropped open. George didn't recognise them but Holly knew who they were. "Grandma! and...Great Grandma Millie! But...?"

"Hello, Holly, Hello George," said the elder of the two. "I'm your Great Grandma Millie. We never met I know, as I came Home long before you were both born." She waved a hand towards Grandma Margot. "We've both been following your visit from a distance. And your lives on Earth too, of course, and both with great pleasure and admiration I might add."

Grandma Margot spoke softly. "Hello, darlings. George, I'm Grandma Margot. You *have* turned out well, you were only just born when I last came back Home, and you, Holly, you must have been about five. We want you to know we're extremely proud of you both. You are growing up into two beautiful, mature young people and we love you very much.

Be good to your Mum and Dad and be kind and supportive to each other, that's all we can ask."

Now it was George's turn to burst into tears. It wasn't that he was unhappy, in fact quite the opposite. It was just that the whole visit had been full of such emotional surprises and now meeting his long-lost Grandmas just overwhelmed him for a few moments. The two old ladies talked with Holly and George for several minutes, reminding them how much they were loved and how much they had to contribute to their more familiar world back on Earth.

"Goodbye, my darlings," said Grandma Margot finally, hugging George and Holly tightly to her and stroking their hair lovingly.

"Goodbye, Holly. Goodbye, George," said Great Grandma Millie, smiling that One Big Happiness smile that Helen had smiled when they had first arrived with Rilke and Tik.

And so it went on as all the Souls said their piece. On more than one occasion Holly found she was crying again too.

"It's okay to cry, beautiful Holly," said Helen soothingly. "It's been so wonderful having you and George up Here with me, I am so blessed that you two are in my lives."

"Will we ever... see you again?" George asked, his

cheeks puffy red and glistening.

"Georgie, we're in the same Soul family. We'll be in and out of each other's lives for the rest of time," Helen assured him tenderly. "I'll be waiting at your next Homecomings, when you've completed your current Life-paths. And you'll see Old Harry, and meet Sophie and Kati, and all your Soul Family and Soul Friends will be here too, waiting to welcome you Home."

"Let me share you again what is for me the two most important things to be rememberin'," offered Old Harry. "First is to choose the best learnin' attitude you think will help you through difficult times, 'cos there certainly be a boatload of those Downstairs. Meetin' all them challenges you's chose Downstairs be powerful tricky at best of times, without you choosin' to be meetin' them in mis'rableness," he added.

"And number two?" asked George.

"Number two what?" asked Old Harry.

"Oh, Harry!" cried Holly. "Your memory is terrible! You said there were two important things to remember, choosing our attitudes and…?"

"So I did, that would be…ah, indeed – to *always* be mindful of any opportunities where you could be hearin' somethin' useful. They can spring out at you at any time,

from any situation or circumstance, long as you's payin'
attention to where they might be."

Teleka seized her chance, and blustered breathlessly in to
the conversation. "Good advice, Harry! And I've got one
too! Be quiet! That's it! Time to be quiet and still is essential
every now and then, away from the hurly-burly of life…and
noisy friends," she announced grandly, making a point of
glancing over at Ponke and Wakke. "That's all that's needed
to ask those soul-searching questions and get in touch with
our secrets."

"That's rich coming from you!" cackled Wakke. "A
foghorn in a fairground is quieter than you!"

"Possibly on the harsh side, Waks, though undoubtedly
poetic," approved Ponke, jovially.

"Now, now, you two, it's a good point, nonetheless,"
smiled Helen, diplomatically. "Make some quiet time
whenever you can to ask your questions, then listen
carefully, and you'll hear us whenever you need to," she
summarised.

"I climb into the Poppy Tree for that," said Holly. "I've
always asked my questions up there."

"Well *my* question is 'What's the secret Magpie's
Secret?'" declared George, doggedly.

Everyone laughed.

"You just keep payin' attention to what comes your way, Master George, keep them eyes and ears open at all times. Answers'll come quicker'n you imagines they will."

Quok had moved over to where George was standing and while everyone was still chattering away to each other, he beckoned to George with his wing to come closer, so he could whisper in his ear.

"You're a special Soul, George, old man, and I'm glad to have made your acquaintance up Here. Would you care to call your charming sister over for a sec, thought I'd just add my tuppence-worth before the two of you take off."

"You want me to…? Holly?" George verified, sensing he had to be quick.

Quok nodded, importantly.

"Hols! Holly!" stage-whispered George to his sister, who was standing a few paces away. She didn't immediately react, so he strode over to her, trying to be casual, yet purposeful at the same time. "Holly, you have to come with me…quickly! And ssshhh!" he warned, putting his finger to his lips, and tugging her sleeve with his free hand.

"What?" said Holly abruptly, a little annoyed at George's insistence.

"Ssshhh, don't say a word, you have to come quickly – Quok wants to say something while no-one's paying attention!"

"Quok? But he…?"

"Come on!"

George led her the few paces to where Quok was standing as nonchalantly as a magpie knows how, waiting for them to approach.

"He *can* speak, Hols, he wants to say something before we go."

Holly looked at Quok, and then at George. She tilted her head slightly to one side and raised her eyebrows quizzically at Quok. Quok motioned with an almost imperceptible wave of his wing for them both to come closer. They took another half step towards him and he began immediately.

"See up there in that tree, that's a great friend of mine, Settika." Quok was careful to cover his beak with his wing, ensuring his words were only audible to his select guests.

Holly was amazed to hear him speak. She craned her head closer.

"Wise old magpie she is," Quok continued conspiratorially. "A tad Old School, perhaps, but one of the few I ever share my own little secret with," he tapped his beak with the tip of his wing. "One always comes away from a tête-à-tête with her knowing something new.

"Now I may be wrong, but my instinct tells me you'll

come away from this little visit with a much broader picture of things, and you'll both be well-equipped to become outstanding teachers in your own ways. The age-old challenge for humans is always that they don't manage to remember much from up Here when they arrive back Downstairs.

"However, Settika over there, has been following your progress from an astute distance, and seems to think you're on the verge of grasping an important point, and I'm inclined to agree with the old hen. It's quite simple really, and she puts it rather nicely, so I thought she'd like me to share it with you. Are you ready to hear it?"

George and Holly nodded dutifully, intrigued.

"Here it is then. Settika said to tell you: `Souls don't much mind what you *do* in your lives, they mind simply what you are *being* when you're *doing* it,'" said Quok. "That's it, in a nutshell – short and sweet. Don't know if it helps any, but believe me when I tell you, my young friends, this is a…"

He stopped himself without finishing his sentence, interrupted by the other magpies bustling around them again.

"Now here's a bird knows about quiet and stillness, isn't that right, Quokky" squawked Ponke, chuckling at his friend. "'Bye, George, 'bye, Holly. You'll see us around!" he called, waving a large wing at them.

"Unless we see you first!" wise-cracked Wakke.

"We'll leave you with Rilke and Tik this time," said Teleka. "You'll be in safe wings. Goodbye! Good luck!"

George was standing very quiet and very still all of a sudden.

"Look at him," screeched Ponke, pointing at George. "Looks like someone pays heed to Teleka's advice after all!"

Holly looked over at George and saw he was peering intently at a nearby tree, squinting up into the branches. She walked over to him and asked him softly, "What is it, Porge? You OK?"

"Hols… Settika, look! In the tree…"

"She's just another magpie, Georgie."

"Quok! Quok!" said Quok, winking slyly in his direction.

"You're unusually talkative all of a sudden," teased Ponke, and then squawked as Teleka clouted him with the heel of her foot.

"Don't be cheeky!" she warned him, ever protective towards Quok, and still smarting from their earlier insolence towards her.

"But that makes seven…" George began, protesting. "Look, Tik, Rilke, Wakke, Ponke, Teleka and Quok… and then…"

He turned back towards the tree only to see the distant

silhouette of Settika flying off into the distance.

"But Quok! When you were saying…what you were saying…she…" and his voice trailed off as he realised that no-one else knew that Quok could speak. The others turned towards him.

"You'll not get much conversation out of him, young George," advised Ponke, solemnly.

"Quok," said Quok, looking straight at George.

"See what we mean!" confirmed Wakke.

"So was that…?" George began, and then gave up. What was it Old Harry had said? Be mindful of any opportunities to hear something useful – they can spring out at you at any time so long as you are paying attention. Had Quok just revealed a secret Magpie Secret? he wondered.

"Come on George - One Big Happiness!" Holly found the words floating into her thoughts and out of her mouth automatically. She noticed everyone around her smiling and nodding.

"You've seen how fabulous it is coming back Home up Here, so what on Earth could there possibly be to be sad about?" asked Grandma Margot, simply.

Holly and George looked at the crowd of beaming Souls waiting to wave them off back to Earth. After all they had seen and heard in their incredible, whirlwind tour of Soul

School, neither could think of a single thing.

Everyone was starting to float back a little way to make space for Rilke and Tik to take off.

"Now it's really time to say goodbye," Helen said. "Be kind to Mum and Dad won't you, they are so lucky to have you with them, they will learn so much from you too!"

Even though I'm only seven? wondered George to himself, realising for the first time that it wasn't necessarily *always* such a good thing to be a grown-up before you're ready. He stepped back onto the magpies' nest alongside Holly. Right on cue, their silver cords materialised from nowhere, and they instinctively grabbed hold of them with one hand, leaving the other free to wave.

"Especially *because* you're only seven, George," laughed Helen out loud, reading George's mind again, "and because you have both chosen wonderful Life-paths to lead this time around. Harry said it was alright to tell you that, but for the rest you will have to wait and see what challenges are in front of you, won't you!"

"Tell me, tell me, *TELL ME! WHAT HAPPENS*??" called George as Rilke and Tik started to flap their strong wings and the nest lifted a few metres off the ground.

"You'll know soon enough," Helen called back, smiling her biggest, lovingest smile as Holly and George were lifted higher and higher. "I will always love you both. Talk to me anytime you need to," she shouted, "and I'll help you find your way. Be happy in your lives down there, just as I am up Here, and some day we will meet up again!"

The large crowd of Souls waved fondly and Holly and George waved back, watching everyone become smaller and more distant.

"*I LOVE YOU TOO*!!!!" shouted Holly at the top of her voice, and even though they were now flying through the skies as fast as lightning she knew that Helen had heard her.

Holly and George clung on to their silver cords as Rilke and Tik flapped their strong wings effortlessly through the skies. Both were trying to remember all of the incredible things that they had just seen and heard and felt and, yes, even smelled. Holly smiled to herself as she remembered the Lemon Drops and Peppermint and Liquorice All-Sorts.

George saw a small white feather in the nest next to his feet, and he picked it up and tickled Holly's neck with it. She, however, was lost in her own thoughts and didn't seem to notice.

Rilke noticed though and called back over her shoulder. "That's one of Tik's. Keep it if you like. Every time you find a feather by itself on Earth…"

"…'Specially a magpie feather," interrupted Tik.

234

"...It means there's a Guide close by, keeping an eye on you, probably reminding you to think about something you need to do," continued Rilke. "And if it's a white one, it'll be an Angel reminding you that you're loved and safe from harm."

George stopped tickling Holly and put the feather in his pocket. He yawned, and blinked several times. He was doing his best to keep his eyes from closing, as he didn't want to miss a second of the amazing ride home.

Inevitably though, the exertions and euphoria of their visit to Soul School were starting to take their toll. Holly tried to work out how long they had been away - was it hours or even a day...or more than that? They had been so busy finding out about Soul School and Life Lessons and Homecomings and Angels and Guides and playing...and they hadn't slept once. In the end she gave up. She simply hadn't a clue how long it had been.

One thought kept insisting it should take pride of place in the front of her mind: from now on she would always try to be happy and positive and open to learning when thinking about meeting difficult challenges, especially the most difficult one of all – coping with the idea of someone who was likely to die or had died.

It's true, she reflected a little sleepily, the dying part is often very painful and traumatic for everyone involved. That part would be a difficult challenge to meet. She could see how it would be an important Life Lesson to try to cope with it as sensitively as possible. But the knowledge that actually *being* dead freed the Soul to come Home for a well-earned rest... well, if these Souls were anything to go by then that wasn't scary at all – on the contrary, it was just - what had Helen called it? – a learning pause, a well-earned, relaxing, learning pause.

She looked over at George. The non-stop exhilaration had exhausted him and he was out for the count - fast asleep standing up in the nest. She remembered Old Harry and Helen telling her she might forget certain parts of the visit to Soul School so she made a conscious effort to fix a beautiful picture in her mind of how happy Helen and all the other Souls had seemed. With that picture she decided to give her eyelids a little rest.

As she let them droop down over her tired eyes, an inevitable wave of drowsiness came over her too. Before she knew it she, like her little brother, was fast, fast asleep as Rilke and Tik flew them back to Earth.

"No 'batics this time then, d'you think, Rilks?" asked Tik of his loyal companion, his powerful wings beating rhythmically with hers.

"Best not, Tikko," Rilke replied, a touch wistfully. "Best let 'em sleep, never seen a pair of mites so pooped."

CHAPTER 21
Back Downstairs

"Hol-ly! Geo-orge!" Dad was calling for them from the French windows. "Where have they got to? Is that you two up in the tree?" He walked into the garden and round to the far side of the tree and peered up into the dusk shadows.

Holly woke first. "What…? Where…?"

"Wake up, Hols, and wake your brother too. Come on, sleepy heads, let's get you inside, we're going to light the candles on Helen's cake."

"Mum said…I could light them," said Holly, drowsily, rubbing her knuckles in her eyes. She pushed George's tousled head away from her shoulder where he'd been resting it and then clambered down the trunk backwards.

"'Course you can," said Dad. "And George can blow them out. Come on, Georgie, wake up, son."

Now it was George's time to open his eyes, and, blinking blearily, he lowered himself carefully off the branch into his Dad's strong arms.

"I know two young people who'll be after an early night," said Dad as they walked back inside to light the candles on Helen's cake.

And, less than twenty minutes later, his prediction was proved absolutely correct.

* * *

Next morning Holly swung her legs out from under her blankets and scrunched her toes into her fluffy pink rabbit slippers as she sat on the edge of her bed. She yawned, stretched and stood up sleepily.

"Hol-ly! Breakfast's ready, darling!" she heard Mum calling up the stairs.

Dozens of thoughts and questions were swirling around in her head as she clumped slowly down the wooden stairs, along the hallway and into the kitchen. Why do I have this strange feeling that something really unusual happened last night? Holly wondered.

As she sat at the table, Mum plonked a glass of pineapple juice down in front of her, followed a minute later by a plate with two boiled eggs in egg-cups and ten bread soldiers. George sat at the other side of the table in his pyjamas. He was lining up his own bread soldiers to attack the runny yellow insides of his decapitated boiled eggs, both of which had fearsome faces drawn on their shells by Dad in felt-tip pen.

Mum sat down next to Holly, reaching over to stroke her daughter's bed-head hair. Unexpectedly, as she did so, her eyes welled up and she started to cry.

"Hey, Bex" said Dad lovingly, "Don't cry. Let poor Hols eat her eggs. Come over here, darling, you need a big hug."

But before her Mum could move, Holly pushed her own chair back and stood up next to her Mum's chair. Without thinking she took her Mum's head in both hands and pulled it close to her own, so their faces were just inches apart.

"It's okay to cry, Mum," she said, entwining her Mum's long brown hair around her fingers. "We're all going to be fine, Dad, you'll see, we're all going to learn to cope with not having Helen around. Helen's happy in Heaven now, and I know she loves us so, so much. She probably only needed to come down for twenty years this time to learn to make us all happy. She won't want us to be crying – she wants us to be hap…"

She stopped talking because she realised that Mum and Dad were both looking at her, and then at each other, in astonishment, their mouths and eyes wide open.

She picked up a bread soldier from her plate, dunked it into her runny egg yolk, then crammed it all into her mouth and chewed it slowly, while her parents stared at her, then at each other, then back at her again.

"We all miss Helen, Mum," she continued, talking through her mouthful. "Life is going to be a big challenge for everybody. It's not easy to learn to cope with everything, but we *can* choose how hard we're going to try," she finished matter-of-factly.

"Holly, darling, where did you learn to think like that…and talk like that?" Dad asked, a little taken aback.

"Mm, dunno," Holly replied, absent-mindedly, munching into another eggy soldier.

"I miss Helen too," piped up George. "I really want her here to play with and to make me laugh, but 'specially because I'm nearly ten, I can play with you instead, if you want."

Mum didn't know whether she was crying or laughing now, hearing the children talking like this, but she felt much calmer anyway.

"George, son, you have to be eight and nine first before you can be ten," Dad smiled lovingly at his son. "So take your time growing up won't you! But one thing is for sure…Mum and I are very lucky to have such special and wise children around."

He leaned over and smothered George in a huge Dad-Hug just as George was about to put another egg soldier in his mouth. The soldier got squashed all over George's chin and the runny yolk dripped on to his pyjama top and left a sticky yellow smudge on Dad's shirt.

"And I'm so happy I chose you for my Mum and Dad too…" said Holly.

"*You*…chose *us*…?!" Mum interrupted, looking over at Dad with a bewildered expression across her face. Dad turned his palms upwards towards the ceiling and shrugged his shoulders.

Holly carried on, without noticing, "…I don't know exactly what's going to happen, but I do know that to find out, we just have to ask the right questions. The Poppy Tree's a good place to go for that. Then if we listen carefully enough we'll know what to do. We can still talk to Helen any time we want, she is always listening, you know."

"Holly, darling, I know you miss your sister," said Dad. "But when I hear you talking like this, well, you sound so…"

"So grown up," finished Mum proudly. "You..."

But Holly was on automatic pilot. "Any time we miss Helen," she interrupted, "we just have to think of a little message and she'll get it in Heaven. Then she can send little messages back to help us do something positive to take our minds off missing her. So the more we miss her the more special things we do, until we just end up doing special things whether we think about missing her or not."

Mum had moved over to sit herself down on Dad's knee

for a hug while Holly was talking. Now she pulled George out of his chair on to her own knee and hugged him tightly too. This time George remembered to leave his egg soldiers on the plate so the yolk didn't go all over everyone. They all sat in silence for a few moments, and then Mum spoke up.

"Oh, Children, you're adorable! I tell you what, as a special treat I'm going to let you both have a day off school. When Dad's gone to work we can all go and do anything you want today – it's your day, OK?"

"Mummy Dummy!" said George, cheekily. "It's the beginning of school mid-term break today, we don't go to school for another week! And Dad's off till Wednesday, aren't you Dad!"

"Is it? Don't you? Are you?" asked Mum, looking very confused.

"He's right, Bex," said Dad, and turned to his children. "Mum's not thinking clearly because it's been such a difficult week for us all."

Mum glanced at the calendar on the wall. "Oh yes, so it is! Well, that's wonderful then!" she beamed. Her face brightened up into a happy smile. "We can all four go out somewhere for the day then. Yes…we'll have a fun family day out, anywhere you choose."

George's face lit up. "Can I finish my egg soldiers first

though?" he asked.

"Of course you can, darling," said Mum "Then go and have a wash and get dressed and have a think about where you want to go."

Twenty minutes later, Holly had arrived back downstairs. She was dressed in her favourite orange flared jeans and the bright pink T-shirt that Helen had painted for her last-but-one birthday with special cloth paint. It said "My Bestest Sis" across the chest in different coloured letters, with a smiley face made from sequins and some hand-painted flowers and birds on the sleeves.

"You look lovely, Holly," smiled Mum. "That's exactly the right outfit to choose for today."

Then George reappeared, wearing exactly the same clothes he'd had on yesterday.

Holly and Mum gave each other a secret, knowing look.

"So have you two decided where you want us to go yet?" asked Mum.

"Water Park!" replied George, excitedly.

"Oh, George, we have to book that a few days in advance, otherwise the queues are just so-o-o long," said Mum, apologetically. "Tell you what. We could book for later in the week if you like, and you can invite a couple of friends too – how does that sound?"

"Too cool!" yelled George, his mind going into immediate overdrive. "We can phone Nathan and Brett and Matty and…"

"Hang on, hang on!" laughed Mum. "We only have one car, not a *minibus*. We'll sit down and work out which *two* of your friends can come with us, OK?"

George knew he'd been trying it on. "OK, Mum," he agreed good-naturedly.

"And you, Hols? What would you like to do today?" Mum asked.

"Mmm, do you mind if we just stay home together today and have a fun family day around here instead?" asked Holly.

"That sounds like a wonderful idea, sweetie," said Mum, "is there anything particular you want to do?"

"Hmmmmmmm," hummed Holly, putting her forefinger on her chin while she thought about it.

"Hmmmmmmm," hummed George, imitating his sister and receiving a playful cuff from her that skimmed the top of his head.

Just for a couple of moments, they looked up simultaneously towards the kitchen ceiling. They both thought they noticed the kitchen light bulb glow really brightly. It was definitely a brighter than usual golden-white glow for about two seconds, and then it was back to normal…or did they imagine it?

All of a sudden both children had firm ideas about what they would do that day.

"I think I'd like to just go to my room and write down some ideas for my school project this morning, Mum. Then…ummm…then this afternoon you can take me shopping!" Holly announced.

"Oh I can, can I?" laughed Mum. "You know when you're onto a good thing, don't you? And you, George?"

"I think I want to go and sit in the Poppy Tree and think about Helen for a while. She'll send me some ideas for special things I can do this week. And then this afternoon Dad can take *me* shopping," declared George.

"Copy Cat!" teased Holly.

"Dopey Dog!" returned George.

"Stop!" yelled Dad, walking back into the kitchen and shaping a letter 'T' with his hands. "Time Out! This house is a Zonk-free zone today…ALL day!" he warned, grinning despite himself, and shaking his forefinger at both of them very unconvincingly.

"Mum…?" started George.

"Yes, hon?"

"…you don't have to watch me through the kitchen

window any more when I'm in the Poppy Tree. I'm a really good climber," George stated firmly.

"How did you know we...?" Mum began, and then stopped. There had been so many surprises this morning already that this latest one didn't really seem to matter. She knelt down in front of her children and put her arms behind their heads. Then she pulled them close towards her, rubbing her nose against theirs in turn, like a family of seals, and planting a wet kiss on each of both their cheeks.

"Yeeuughhh!" groaned George, loving it, really. He wiped his face with the back of his hand. "And Dad...?"

"What is it, son?"

"I'm going to be World Champion at kite-surfing when I grow up."

"Kite-surfing??!!" exclaimed Dad, raising his left eyebrow, quizzically at his wife. "Where did...?"

Mum interrupted. "I think that's a wonderful idea, George darling," she said, with a happy, loving smile lighting up her face. "Now off you go up that tree, and we promise not to watch from the window!" she smiled at Dad. "Oh, and here," she took a small plastic bag from the wall cupboard and handed it to him. "Take some Liquorice All-Sorts with you in case you get peckish."

"Thanks, Mum!" George's face lit up too. She didn't

normally allow sweets so soon after breakfast. He squashed the bag into his jeans pocket.

"George…?" began Holly, as her brother walked towards the back door.

"Mm?" George half turned.

"Can I have a sweet before you go?" she asked, winking mischievously at Mum. "One of the yellow round ones with the black in the middle."

George hesitated, looking suspiciously at his sister. "But you don't even *like* Liquorice All-Sorts," he replied guardedly.

"I like yellow round ones with the black in the middle," said Holly, evenly.

George looked at his sister and then at Mum, who was trying to hide a smile, as she too knew how hard it was to get George to part with his sweets. He reluctantly pulled the bag out of his pocket and looked inside to see if he could find one (and *only* one) yellow round one with the black in the middle. His eyes fell on two at the bottom of the bag. Carefully, shielding the bag from his sister, he took one out between his thumb and forefinger, and put it into Holly's outstretched palm.

"There's only one," he lied.

"Thanks, Bruv!" Holly smiled triumphantly towards

Mum. "*Too* kind!"

Mum, who was bending down to pick something up, shot her daughter a warning 'don't-push-your-luck' sort of glance.

"Here, Georgie Porge, this fell out of your pocket when you pulled out the sweets," she said, standing up. She handed him a small white feather she'd picked up off the floor. "Tell Helen that we all love her very, very much, won't you," she instructed him, as he opened the kitchen door into the garden.

George took the feather and turned, absent-mindedly stroking himself under the chin a couple of times with it.

"She knows," he said simply, and walked out into the garden, shutting the door behind him.

THE

~~END~~

...BEGINNING

An interview with the Author

Where did the idea for this book come from?

JMW　　　Life is, as they say, a fatal condition. As we get older, the health of even the most robust of us eventually succumbs and we all inevitably die. Children generally accept this as a logical sequence, so answering their questions concerning death in older or ill people is relatively straightforward.

However, try explaining the deaths of younger people to them - sudden or unexpected deaths, tragic accidents or violent deaths – it's far less clear-cut. And it was after the deaths of my sister, my fiancée and a number of young friends that I felt I needed to explore my deeper responses. To make sense of these seemingly senseless events, it's all too easy to colour the subsequent grieving response with anger, resentment, depression, denial, blame or bitterness. All of these inhibit acceptance of the loss, sometimes permanently.

What did you find when you explored your own responses?

JMW　　　I found that I was actually quite accepting of these deaths, comparatively speaking, despite the youth of those who died, although I wasn't entirely sure where that acceptance emanated from, nor if I should be happy with it. But I found other's reactions compounded and blended any number of negative emotions into all areas of their lives, often resulting in chronic sabotage to their own and others' well being.

The 'normality' of reactions like theirs seem to be further

reinforced by relentless and sensationalist media stories and literature. And that's just the adults – us adults who are supposed to have more experience at coping with the world we inhabit.

So where did the idea for making 'Seven for a Secret' accessible to children come from?

JMW   It is a short step for these negative coping strategies to filter down to children. Children all too naturally absorb and re-create the adults' fears, half-truths and destructive behaviour, often with devastating consequences for later life. I couldn't find any literature specifically aimed at young people that combined their inevitable questions about dying with a forward-looking sense of empowerment.

So I decided to combine the messages of making one's own choices and accepting oneself, essentially what has come to be called life coaching, with the implications of not judging others for their choices or becoming over-emotive towards the challenges faced by those apparently less fortunate than ourselves. Then I put it in a language that I hope is accessible and inspiring to young readers, as a story.

The idea of writing a children's book about death isn't new, although combining it with what you term 'positive grieving' is less common.

JMW   True, and that's where I believe we need to make the most headway because children and young people are capable of understanding so much more than the confused mish-mash of euphemistic messages that are programmed into them currently. The fact that this story doesn't fit into mainstream western religious thinking is the whole point of writing it.

How do you see western grief culture now?

JMW   Happily, western grief culture has come a long way over the last thirty years and many people are very enlightened, having chosen to leave behind the repressive seedbeds of agitation and negativity found in the past. There's still some ground to cover though and I want this book to provoke discussion and challenge people to examine what they would like to feel after the death of a loved one.

What is your vision of the way forward with regard to making the positive grief process accessible to young people?

JMW   Well it's not only the young I'd like to encourage to think in a more open-minded way, because it's the adults who have often been entrenched in narrow religious and cultural belief structures for so long that the majority of their responses come from outside of themselves. But I'd like to think that '**Seven for a Secret**' conjures up a world, regardless of one's religion or belief system, in which young people can fully grasp the intertwined concepts of life, death and fulfilment of purpose.

Personally I'd like to embrace a world in which young people can confidently discuss their insights around the implications of reincarnation with brothers and sisters, friends and parents over the dinner table. I'd like to envision a world in which parents are relieved of the burden of awkward, inadequate and 'diplomatic' explanations surrounding death, and can answer their children's questions effortlessly. And I suppose finally I'd like to anticipate a world in which schools infuse the philosophies of positive grieving, of boldly meeting challenges and choosing one's attitudes into the eager, open minds of the young.

So in a nutshell, you imagine a world in which all children could grow up this way?

JMW   Exactly! Good Grief - what a great gift!

Reviews

I was slightly concerned about what I would find when I started to read this book. Having worked with many dying children and their families, I wondered what this book might contribute, how it would be pitched and used.. I was delighted with it's message, full of hope, love and potential, not only for children/ young people/ any individual facing death or grieving, but with opportunity to adopt skills for a less than perfect life, laced with challenge, loss and surprises... An excellent tool for any professional working directly with children, carers, parents, guardians... a treasure.

Angela Stephen

The bravery of it! At last someone with personal experience of bereavement has put pen to paper to share a descriptive view of what happens to that spark, which is life, once our physical being fails.

All those involved in bereavement counselling, schools, parents and children of an age where they are beginning to explore the written word, should read Seven for a Secret. Where else will you find such a tangible description of what, until now, has almost been treated as a taboo?

James Mackenzie Wright treads carefully not to cause alienation to those of any particular religious belief, tackling a subject that up to press has been the sole domain of religious doctrine.

Maybe I was already prejudiced to accept the concept. From a very young age I have always believed that "life" as I call it, the "Soul" as James sees it, cannot just disappear. The coalescing of souls, the "Sea of Souls" will bring new comfort for those trying to make sense of the awful apparent permanence of the loss of someone they love.

I applaud James for being brave enough to write "Seven for a Secret" and for adopting a writing style that transcends age, religion, sex and race. I just hope that in the years to come we will also be able to applaud all those who are enlightened enough to encourage everyone they know to pick up this book, read it, delight in it and inevitably cry, in the relief and the hope that comes with the realisation that after all there is a point to it all.

David Roberts

I approached this book expecting it to be a vehicle for a child. I was charmed and delighted to find that as an adult, it had universal appeal and was one of the most accessible books that I have read. The language is easy on the mind and the idea is clear, non-dictatorial and does not leave one with the feeling of sensationalism that many books which deal with this subject matter often do.

The author's belief is that the soul never dies, but lives through a series of 'life lessons' in order to experience and grow. The idea is both comforting and plausible and I feel that this book could be of real benefit to those who are recently bereaved or who are suffering with terminal illness, either personally or with a loved one.

I would like to see this book on the shelves of every school and believe that adults and children alike would benefit from it's serene message. It would be a helpful aid in group discussion, preferably with adults and children present. In this world of confusion and conflict, I found it a little oasis of relief and my children are absorbed in it too.

Lynda Sanderson

Seven for a Secret is "for inquisitive minds seeking to make sense of the world in which they live." I found it delivers amazing insights on life and death. The author has written in open dialogue to help us reach our own conclusions and choices. This is a thought provoking book for everyone - dealing with life, illness and death issues. It is a valuable piece of writing or "story" that I shall be recommending to others and keeping for my young family. Every time I see a magpie I smile!

Lyn Wesemael

A visionary and sensitive book dealing with the little discussed area of child bereavement. It is an enchanting story which every family should read when faced with a life threatening illness or bereavement, as my own has been a number of times.

Carol Wilson

A book about managing bereavement written in a fun and mischievous way? I expected a vehicle for children but was charmed to find it is one of the most accessible and universal books in this genre that I have encountered.

"Seven for a Secret" is essentially a fantasy novel, written in delightful, cheeky prose (reminiscent of Alice in Wonderland) where two young children are whisked away by some raucous magpies and reunited with their sister who had died a year earlier. She introduces them to many fun characters in Soul School, who provide wise and challenging pointers around death, life and fulfilment of purpose. "Life coaching meets death coaching" if you like.

A tantalising thread of reincarnation weaves through every chapter - a brave choice of backdrop, and portrayed beautifully to allow the story come alive - whether it's "true" or not doesn't matter one bit – it works, it's comforting and it feels great!

Encourage everyone you know to pick up this visionary and sensitive book and revel in the realisation that there is, after all, a point in being here.

Soul & Spirit, March 2008

Michelle Pridmore

Seven For A Secret

Seven For A Secret

Seven For A Secret

Seven For A Secret

Seven For A Secret

Seven For A Secret

Seven For A Secret

Seven For A Secret

Seven For A Secret

Seven For A Secret

Seven For A Secret

Seven For A Secret

Seven For A Secret

Seven For A Secret

Seven For A Secret

Seven For A Secret